P9-BAW-505

RUNNER

THIS IS A BORZOI BOOK PUBLISHED BY ALFRED A. KNOPF

This is a work of fiction. Names, characters, places, and incidents either are the product of the author's imagination or are used fictitiously. Any resemblance to actual persons, living or dead, events, or locales is entirely coincidental.

Copyright © 2007 by Robert Newton

All rights reserved.
Published in the United States by Alfred A. Knopf, an imprint of Random House Children's Books, a division of Random House, Inc., New York.

KNOPF, BORZOI BOOKS, and the colophon are registered trademarks of Random House, Inc.

www.randomhouse.com/teens

Educators and librarians, for a variety of teaching tools, visit us at www.randomhouse.com/teachers

Library of Congress Cataloging-in-Publication Data

Newton, Robert.
Runner / Robert Newton. — 1st ed.
p. cm.
SUMMARY: In Richmond, Australia, in 1919, fifteen-year-old Charlie Feehan becomes an errand boy for a notorious mobster, hoping that his ability to run will help him, his widowed mother, and his baby brother to escape poverty.
ISBN 978-0-375-83744-9 (trade) — ISBN 978-0-375-93744-6 (lib. bdg.)
[1. Running—Fiction. 2. Poverty—Fiction. 3. Mothers and sons—Fiction. 4. Organized crime—Fiction. 5. Richmond (Vic.)—Fiction. 6. Australia—History—1901–1922—Fiction.] I. Title.
PZ7.N4872Ru 2007
[Fic]—dc22
2006029275

Printed in the United States of America

April 2007

10 9 8 7 6 5 4 3 2 1

First American Edition

For Poppy

RUNNER
ROBERT NEWTON

COCHRAN PUBLIC LIBRARY
174 BURKE STREET
STOCKBRIDGE, GA 30281

Alfred A. Knopf

New York

HENRY COUNTY LIBRARY SYSTEM
MCDONOUGH, STOCKBRIDGE, HAMPTON,
LOCUST GROVE, FAIRVIEW

HENRY COUNTY LIBRARY SYSTEM
McDONOUGH, STOCKBRIDGE, HAMPTON,
LOCUST GROVE, FAIRVIEW

RUNNER

CHAPTER ONE

Richmond, Melbourne, 1919

That day, I recall, was the start of the rain.

Overnight, huge menacing clouds thundered into town and set up camp above the city. In the morning, while my baby brother slept, Ma and I stood on the front porch gazing up at the dirty black sky. Next door, too, our old neighbor, Cecil Redmond, had his eyes raised skyward.

"Have ya ever seen anythin' so black, Mr. Redmond?" called Ma.

"Indeed I 'ave, missus," he replied. "Just now, when the good wife smiled at me."

In the seedy streets of Richmond, you would not find two finer neighbors than the Redmonds, and, if truth be known, they were more like grandparents to my brother and me. Still, Mr. Redmond was right. His wife's rotting teeth were sadly in need of attention.

"There's no money in the purse," he continued, "but I know the fang farrier who works on the 'orses' teeth at the track. I'm told 'e does 'ouse calls on weekends."

Smiling, I lifted my coat collar about my ears.

"Ya need not smile, Charlie," whispered Ma as she kissed my cheek. "He needs little encouragement. Ya'd best be off ta school."

I braced myself against the weather and stepped off the porch.

"Remember what I said now," she called after me as I headed out the gate. "Sit at the front. Ya'll learn nothin' with the daydreamers down the back."

"A course, Ma," I lied. "Front row, nice and close."

At the gate I turned right into Cubitt Street and headed toward school. Straightaway, the icy southerly fixed me for an easy target and began whistling through the holes in my ragged coat. By the time I'd reached the end of the street, it was inside me, laughing, feeding off my bones.

Let me tell you, I was no stranger to the cold, but neither were we friends. It paid little to be on speaking terms with such a monster, for I'd seen what it could do firsthand as my father lay in bed, coughing blood until he died.

Warmth.

That was what the poor craved most in the winter months, but without money we seldom found it. In the slums of Richmond, it was dampness was the enemy. It moved into houses, rising in the walls, black and wet, like a cancer.

Some families with sick children had little choice but to take to their own houses, stripping bits of wood from the floor inside, just for a few minutes of flame each night. By the end of the winter, there'd be nothing left to walk on at all.

To be poor was to be cold. The two were the same.

But me, I refused to let it take me.

So one day I plotted a course—a simple rectangle of main streets it was, covering only a few miles in distance.

And that very night, when I felt the cold, dull ache in my

bones, I headed out into the dark, damp streets of Richmond, and . . . I ran.

I ran one lap, then two, then three.

I ran until there was nothing left, then fell, smiling, in a crumpled heap at the corner of our street. For a long time I sat there, watching as each steaming breath disappeared into the cold night air. If anyone had seen me, they would surely have thought me mad.

Charlie Feehan's the name, I would have said. *I may be poor, but I sure as 'ell ain't cold.*

After that first night, I took to the streets like a drunk takes to the bottle. I swallowed them up. I drank in every step until the few short miles I'd plotted no longer satisfied my ferocious appetite. I needed more, and my legs delivered. One night, without warning, they took me off course and carried me far afield. They hurled me down seedy back lanes, over bridges, and into the lights of the city itself.

I was unstoppable.

Whooping and hollering, I dodged drunks and played with cars. I jumped over puddles and raced alongside grinding trams.

For hours I ran, until my body burned and the shirt on my back was wet.

Then somehow, after all the twists and turns, my legs found their way back to Cubitt Street and slowed to a walk. As I shuffled toward home, away from the magic of the city and its spells, a horrible burning pain moved into my feet as my father's boots tore the skin from my toes.

Left, right, left, right, left, right.

He had given me the boots as I sat for the last time on his

bed and listened to the wheeze and crackle in his chest. After all those years, that was all he'd had to give.

Over the following months, those shoddy boots tasted the dirt and grime of many streets. True, it was the warmth I sought each night I headed out. It was the prickle of skin and the sweat on my brow. But soon there was something more. The sleazy streets seduced me, and, like a moth to the flame, I gladly surrendered.

At school I quickly grew bored with my books. I abandoned my seat at the front and joined the daydreamers down at the back. I dreamt of Bourke Street with its flashing theater signs, BIJOU and GAIETY, and the sly grog joints and brothels of Little Lonsdale. I had no interest in mathematics or comprehension anymore. Nothing stirred in my head when Mrs. Nagle gave us a verse from the school reader. The street was my classroom now, and I was a student eager to learn.

CHAPTER TWO

So then, it may come as little surprise when I tell you that I headed not to the school on the day I left my ma on the front porch. I turned right instead and made my way to Darlington Parade, for an appointment with Squizzy Taylor.

I knew Darlington Parade well, and after a short walk I found myself outside number eighteen. I rapped on the door and waited.

"Charlie Feehan," I said to the familiar face that answered. It was Dasher Heeney. "I've an appointment ta see Mr. Taylor."

"Yer the last of 'em," replied Dasher. "Come through. Mr. Taylor'll be with ya shortly."

To my surprise, three other boys of similar age to myself were waiting nervously in the front room. I sat and said nothing.

From his pocket, Dasher retrieved a bright red sash and tossed it into my lap.

"Giddyup, Charlie Feehan."

I looked around at the others and noticed each one of them wore a different-colored sash.

Blue. Green. Yellow.

I followed suit and slipped the red sash onto my right arm.

Somewhere inside the house, a door opened to the sound

of laughter and clinking glass. Not long after, the tiny frame of Squizzy Taylor appeared at the door. He was dressed for an outing in a black overcoat with velvet collar, bowler hat, fawn gloves, and pointed leather shoes. In his right hand he carried a cane with a silver knob.

"Mornin', lads." He smiled, flashing a gold tooth.

I sat terrified as he moved into the room with Dasher Heeney by his side.

"Christ! They ain't exactly what ya'd call thoroughbreds, Dasher," he said, inspecting us. "On yer feet, lads, if ya will."

As he walked down the line, Squizzy gave us the once-over. Blue, green, yellow, then red. I tell you, it was as if he'd just stepped into the mounting yard on race day. He stopped in front of me and looked down at my boots.

"'Ave ya ever seen so many 'oles before, Dasher?"

"Indeed I 'ave, Squiz. In the prosecution's case when they tried ta fix ya fer that bank job in Balaclava."

"What's yer name, son?" asked Squizzy.

"Charlie Feehan, sir," I croaked.

"And what's that yer've got stuffed in them boots?"

"It's newspaper, Mr. Taylor."

"Newspaper? D'ya 'ear that, Dasher? Young Charlie 'ere 'as the newspaper fillin' the 'oles in 'is boots. It's the *Herald*, is it, Charlie?"

"It is, sir."

"Very clever, lad. Personally, I've only thought ta wipe me arse with it, but per'aps I've been a bit narrow in me thinkin'."

As Squizzy stepped to the center of the room, we were joined by maybe fifteen men. One of them carried a board with colors down the left and odds to the right.

Blue	4–1
Green	6–1
Yellow	Evens
Red	10–1

Granted, I'd only received my summons to race a day ago when Dasher blocked my path as I hurtled down Flinders Lane. Still, ten to one seemed a bit rough.

It had to be the boots.

Pushing the odds from my mind, I looked around the room and noticed a picture hanging on the wall in front of me. It was a portrait of Squizzy Taylor himself. I fixed my eyes on it as Dasher explained the morning's program.

Some people, it is said, are cursed with a face only their mother could love. And to be honest, Squizzy's portrait did him no favors. When he had spoken to me just now in person, I found him not in the least bit unsightly. However, on the canvas, he looked like a weasel, cunning and beady-eyed.

To be fair, perhaps it was the light.

According to Dasher, each of us was to be given a parcel, slightly smaller than a jewelry box in size, the contents of which were described simply as "delicate." Our task—blue, green, yellow, and red—was to deliver the parcel, undamaged, to a nominated address that would be revealed seconds before the start.

The rules?

There were none.

We were here to run, winner take all.

"So, lads," announced Dasher, "I suggest ya prepare yerselves fer battle."

Next he addressed the men in the room.

"Gentlemen!" he roared. "Place yer bets."

Already near the front, Squizzy threw me a wink and dug his hand into a pocket.

"Dasher, me good man, I'll 'ave a fiver on the red."

While my fellow competitors stood bouncing on their toes, I busied myself pushing bits of newspaper back into the holes in my boots. At evens, all the smart money was coming for yellow. And let me tell you, had I fancied a wager myself, it's where my money would have been. Still, I felt no shame in being the underdog. After all, it was what I knew best.

I was busy tightening the laces on my left boot when a pair of legs appeared in front of me. I kept my head down and peered forward. Straightaway I knew the owner of those muscular legs would be the yellow boy.

"Me name's Barlow," he said. "Jimmy Barlow. Where'd they find *you?*"

I said nothing.

"Ya know, if you was a horse, they'd put a bullet in yer 'ead. Put ya outta yer misery. No wonder no one's backed ya."

"No one except Mr. Taylor," I said.

"Yeah, well, if ya know what's good fer ya, ya'll keep outta me way. Ya got that?"

After the bets were laid, the runners were called.

"Time, lads!" yelled Dasher.

Accompanied by the throng of punters and a haze of cigarette smoke, we shuffled nervously into the hallway and out the front door. At the gate, most of the men gathered around Barlow, hitting him with boozy-breathed advice, strong enough

to fell a fully grown stallion. Blue and green had their admirers, too, but me, I had but one—all five foot two of him. Although he was small in stature, if I had to choose, it was Squizzy I wanted in my corner, above all the others. I'd heard that he was a man not to be trusted—a scheming blaggard who'd squeal on his mother to save his own skin. But already I liked him. There was something about him I admired. Pint-sized and snappily dressed, Squizzy Taylor commanded respect. And what's more, he got it.

He sidled up and fixed me with his piercing brown eyes.

"I reckon I need me 'ead read," he said. "I don't know what it is about ya, lad, but somethin' tells me yer the one."

Over my right shoulder, I snuck another look at Barlow and his rowdy entourage.

"I'll do me best, Mr. Taylor."

"Don't worry 'bout that lot," said Squizzy with a shake of his head. "When it comes ta studyin' the form, they're like a mob a bloody sheep. Not a brain between 'em. Just go like the clappers, son."

Right then an almighty thunderclap exploded overhead, so loud it made each of us drop a few feet closer to the ground. It was only Squizzy who remained standing erect.

"Ain't much point duckin'." He smiled. "Me arse is near touchin' the ground as it is."

As the rest of us straightened up, the heavens opened and dropped a load so vicious, had I closed my eyes, I would have sworn we were being pelted with stones.

"I'm 'opin' ya like a wet track, lad?" asked Squizzy.

"Wet or dry, Mr. Taylor. It don't matter."

Satisfied, Squizzy turned and made his way to the shelter of

the verandah and, true to form, the others followed like sheep. While the punters huddled together, us runners stood ready in a line of four, shivering. A blond woman, heavily made up, appeared from the house carrying a tray of different-colored parcels and handed them to Squizzy.

"Awright, lads," he announced, moving to the front of the verandah. "It's race time! On this 'ere tray are the parcels—blue, green, yellow, and red. Inside each of 'em are two eggs, generously donated by our friends at the Victoria Market."

A heckler at the rear interrupted. "Pull the other one, Squiz. I nicked 'em meself last night."

With a wave of his hand, Squizzy smiled, then continued.

"Like I said, expertly thieved from a Toorak toff's fowl 'ouse. Dolly and meself 'ave a taste fer omelettes tonight, lads, so if ya don't mind, I'll be needin' 'em back in one piece. On each a them parcels is written the same address. Be the first runner to deliver yer parcel ta that said establishment with two eggs unbroken and the race is yers. And if I get word that one a ya was 'itchin' a ride on the sideboard of a tram, I'll give ya a back'ander at the other end. All right, step forward, lads."

Blue. Green. Yellow. Red.

I was the last in line.

As soon as the parcel hit my hand, I looked for the address. 200 Bourke Street, Melbourne.

Immediately I knew it to be the Orient—a popular drinking den where a criminal record guaranteed you entry.

Slowly I shuffled back into line, but already my mind was racing. At night when I ran, it was my legs that steered me. They sent me exploring, in search of new things. But today, it

was different. Today was about winning, and to do that I needed to be clever—clever and fast.

From Darlington Parade, Richmond, to Bourke Street, Melbourne, I would be running in a northwesterly direction, no more than three miles. A sprint. There were shortcuts to be had, back lanes aplenty, but what I needed was space. I plotted the course in my head, favoring the main streets wherever possible. After all, there was Squizzy's dinner to consider. I pictured myself almost there, with the Orient in sight, when a familiar voice brought me back to Darlington Parade. It was Dasher.

"Hold the line, lads, yer in the starter's 'ands."

Teeth chattering, I stood with the others out by the front gate. I looked down at the red parcel in my hand and noticed the rain had washed the address clean away.

"Cripes, I've fergotten the address," whispered Blue Boy next to me. "Was it two hundred or three?"

"Two," I replied.

"Thanks."

Suddenly a howling wind sprang up, grabbed hold of the rain, and pushed it sideways. Icy water stung my right cheek like a slap in the face.

"Take yer marks!"

Four feet pushed forward to the line.

"Get set! . . . Go!"

Three colors broke the line.

I would have been with them had Barlow not dragged me off balance.

I fell awkwardly onto the wet ground and watched the others sprint away.

On the verandah they held their glasses aloft and cheered.

"Yer on a winner there, Squiz!" someone shouted.

Quickly I picked myself up and ran. Out of the corner of my eye I spotted a tiny figure seated in a blue Buick. At first I thought it was a child, what with how low he sat in the passenger seat, but when he dipped his hat and smiled, I knew it was Squizzy.

"Ya'd better get goin', Charlie Feehan," he yelled. "And watch them eggs."

I got goin' all right.

Left, right, left, right, left, right.

Each time my feet hit the ground, they sent a splash of water up around my ankles. I stuffed the eggs into my coat pocket and called on my arms for assistance. Legs are important in a sprint, but you cannot hope to run fast without your arms.

Nearing the end of Darlington Parade, I saw two runners turn left, opting for a shortcut through the gardens. It was a big mistake. I knew from experience that a runner with worn soles on his boots got little purchase on the wet grass—it was another reason I fancied the streets. I left them to it and turned right into Rotherwood Street.

My only thought now was to catch the runner ahead. My legs knew well enough what to do; after all, they'd carried me plenty of times before. So instead, I busied my eyes. I looked for cracks in the pavement. I looked for horses and carts, bicycles, cars, and people—anything that might hinder my progress. Running at speed, in the wet, you needed to be on your toes.

With every step, I made up ground on the runner in front, and soon I was close enough to see the colored sash on his arm.

Yellow.

Barlow was thinking smart. For a brief moment I lost him

as he tackled a bend and headed to Bridge Road. At the corner, he slowed a little and looked back. He was tiring. I was close enough to see his eyes. He was scared. I moved up behind him and sat just off his right shoulder and listened. His breath was long and labored. His feet, instead of lightly tapping the ground, had lost their spring and were crashing heavily into puddles underfoot. All of a sudden the favorite didn't look so good.

I moved up beside him and smiled.

"How's it goin', Barlow?"

"Bugger off."

I must admit, catching Barlow had taken its toll on me, so for a while I was more than happy to match him stride for stride. I settled on his outside, eased back, and found a rhythm. Together we turned left at the Mountain View Hotel and ran, side by side, over Church Street. A dozing mutt, woken by the sound of approaching footsteps, scooted through a front gate and began nipping at our heels. Then, just when I thought Barlow was finished, he seemed to find something. Soon Bridge Road became Wellington Parade, and as we veered right, Barlow ran wide. Before I knew what was happening, he dropped his shoulder and sent me careening into the path of a brown Chrysler.

"You play nice now!" he screamed.

Strangely enough, in the seconds before the car swerved around me and skidded out of control, it was not my own safety that crossed my mind, but that of the eggs. Arms flailing, I tried desperately to stay upright, but I knew I was gone. I flew forward and put my hands out to break the fall. On my hands and knees I skidded across the road, the rough surface tearing my skin as I went. In the middle of the road I came to a halt and propped on all fours. I tell you, if it wasn't for the eggs, I would have lain down across the tram tracks awhile. With blood trickling from my knees, I picked myself up and hobbled off down Wellington Parade. I dared not look at my hands, for the pain told me they were bad. Instead, I thought about the muscles in my legs and made them strong.

Left, right, left, right. *Splish, splash, splish, splash.*

To my surprise, Barlow was still in sight. Down near the Treasury Gardens he was, with Parliament House up ahead.

I still had a chance.

I turned my bloody palms upward to the soothing rain and legged it. As I approached the city, the crowds started to thicken. Dodging and weaving were my specialty, but after my fall I had not the strength, nor the time, for fancy footwork. Instead, I changed my line, stepped into the empty gutter, and ran.

Approaching the Spring Street intersection, I saw the blue and green runners some ten feet to my right. My options were few. I could play it safe and wait for a break in the traffic. Or . . .

Like a madman I threw myself across the intersection, between tooting cars, and made it to the other side. I stepped into the Spring Street gutter and ran.

Had blue and green come, too?

I wasted no time in looking back. It was Barlow I was after. Parliament House, at the top of the city, signaled Bourke Street, so I swung left into the home straight. Eyes peeled, I continued running in the gutter and spotted Barlow battling the crowded footpath. The Orient was fast approaching, and I knew well that time was against me.

I was gaining. Fast.

The path ahead looked clear, so I tucked my head and bolted. Twenty yards became fifteen. Fifteen became ten. I was near flying.

Five yards.

Barlow was almost there. As he raised his hand to the door, he turned and saw me lunging. Too late. Together we fell through the door and crashed to the ground in a heap, much to the delight of the crowded bar.

"Who got up?" someone asked, turning to Dasher.

"Yellow, by a short 'alf 'ead!"

The din in the bar was deafening, and while the favorite was helped to his feet, I picked myself up, unaided, and noticed Squizzy sitting on a stool at the end of the bar.

"Not so fast, gents," he said. "Are ya not fergettin' somethin'?"

"Fergettin' somethin'?" asked Dasher. "Like what?"

"The eggs, Dasher, the eggs."

Another cheer went up as blue and then green pushed their way through the front door.

"Nice of ya ta join us, lads," said Dasher. "How's 'bout we all 'and over them parcels."

The four of us did as we were told, and soon the four colored parcels were lined up across the bar.

"Okay, gents, 'ere we go," said Dasher, unwrapping the blue parcel. "We 'ave, in the blue parcel . . . two eggs, unbroken. Well done, lad."

Blue Boy looked happy.

Next was green.

"The green runner," said Dasher, "has likewise presented two eggs in good workin' order."

Yellow.

The crowd moved in as Dasher unwrapped Barlow's parcel. I could not bear to look, so I dropped my eyes to the floor and stared at the bloodstained newspaper in my boots.

"Give me room, please, gents," barked Dasher. "Yellow, and first past the post, 'as delivered two eggs . . . in an unfit state!"

A groan of disappointment filled the bar.

That left just red.

As Dasher unwrapped my parcel, I turned to Squizzy, who shot me a wink from the end of the bar.

"The red runner," announced Dasher, "at ten ta one, 'as delivered two eggs . . . *unbroken!*"

I'd won.

As the punters turned back to their drinks, muttering in disappointment, Squizzy rose from his stool and moved beside me.

"Don't let on, Charlie Feehan," he whispered, "but yer eggs— I 'ard-boiled 'em meself this mornin'. Welcome aboard, lad."

Bloodied and bruised, I left the warmth of the Orient and stepped outside into the Bourke Street rain. Had I been able, I would have run, but I knew my legs well enough not to ask for anything more. I must have looked a sight, hobbling through the crowd of workers without a brolly. Every inch of me was wet. My only shelter from the rain was a soggy cap, but now it hung so lifeless it was as if I had a cabbage leaf on top of my head.

Normally I would have felt uneasy, limping through the city streets in the daylight hours. Without an adult escort, I was fair game to be collared by a truant officer. But today, I felt different. Today, although my victory had not been entirely aboveboard, I had joined the ranks of the gainfully employed. I was one of them.

At the top end of Bourke Street, I heard a familiar voice close behind me.

"Thanks fer that back there," it said.

Smiling, Blue Boy moved up beside me.

"No worries," I replied.

"Fair dinkum, I'd ferget me own 'ead if it weren't joined ta me neck," he continued. "Still, if it went missin', I don't reckon I'd miss it much."

I turned right at Spring Street, and Blue Boy stepped with me.

"Me name's Norman," he said. "Norman Heath. But people call me Nostrils, on account a me big nose."

"Charlie," I said, offering my hand. "Charlie Feehan."

"Ya sure can run, Charlie Feehan," said Norman. "And let me tell ya, after today, ya'll need ta be fast. D'ya know who it was ya just beat back there?"

"Who? Barlow?"

"Yeah. Yer've 'eard a the Barlows, ain't ya, Charlie? His old man runs the boxin' gym in Fitzroy. Jimmy's got four brothers, and they're mad bastards, the lot of 'em. Even 'is ma. She's got a right hook'd put a grown man ta sleep. You wanna watch yerself, Charlie."

"Did ya ever think ta tell me this before we raced?"

"Not when I got a look at them shoes of yers, I didn't. Yer was ten ta one, remember? How was I ta know ya could run?"

Something didn't add up.

"Tell me somethin', Nostrils," I asked. "If Barlow's from Fitzroy, how come 'e's runnin' for a job in Richmond?"

"I dunno. I 'eard Squizzy's branchin' out. Expandin'. Maybe that's it?"

"Yeah, maybe."

Since my father's death, I'd spent most of my spare time alone. It was easier that way. In the streets, well-meaning neighbors bailed me up and forced me to listen to their stories. *He was a good man, Charlie . . . a fine man.*

Everywhere I went, every corner I turned, someone wanted my ear. It got so that I began feeling awkward, even with my own friends. I avoided the local haunts and hangouts—I even compiled a list of excuses just in case someone came calling at our door.

But with Nostrils it was different. Nostrils was someone new, something fresh. He didn't know my father, and although we'd only just met, I found myself drawn to him.

When we reached Wellington Parade, however, it was time for us to part.

"Remember what I said, now, Charlie. Watch yer back."

"I will, Nostrils. And thanks fer the warnin'. . . . Listen, I don't suppose you and yer nose are doin' anythin' on Sund'y, are ya?"

"Not that I know of. Why?"

"I thought maybe the three of us could go down ta Barkly Gardens and kick the footy. Say two o'clock, my place?"

"Two o'clock? We'll be there."

"Awright, then. It's number seven Cubitt Street. Think ya can remember that, Nostrils?"

"Seven Cubitt, ya said? Let's see . . . seven is Vic Thorp's number—'e's fullback fer the Tigers. No worries. It's only when the numbers get big it's a problem."

Alone, I limped up Punt Road while Nostrils continued up Bridge. I hadn't the heart to tell him that it should have been him on Squizzy Taylor's payroll. Had my eggs not been hard-boiled, I have no doubt they would have arrived at the Orient scrambled, and that result would have disqualified me and handed the title to Nostrils himself. But life was like that sometimes. In the Richmond slums, good fortune was as hard to find as an honest copper. It resided mostly in the leafy suburbs like Brighton and Toorak. So, for boys like me, when good fortune came knocking at your door, you had little choice but to grab it by the scruff of the neck and keep your trap firmly shut.

CHAPTER THREE

Two doors from our house in Cubitt Street, I could hear my brother, Jack, crying inside. While the well-to-do filled their grand houses with music, Ma and I, along with half the neighborhood, made do with the piercing screams of hungry babies.

Next door, Mr. Redmond was out on his porch again, watching the sky. Seeing me, he smiled.

"He's a decent set a lungs on 'im, that brother a yers. A Tiger supporter, I'd say."

There was only one thing that excited Mr. Redmond more than the weather, and that was the Richmond football club.

"I don't reckon 'e'll 'ave much choice if yer've got anythin' ta do with it," I said.

"Yer right there, Charlie."

Behind him, Mrs. Redmond appeared at the door with something in her hands.

"Hello, Charlie," she said, joining her husband. "I've a bowl a broth 'ere fer young Jack. Would ya mind?"

Shivering, I pushed through the gate and approached the porch.

"Crikey, lad," said Mr. Redmond. "What've ya been up ta? Yer bleedin'."

In my hands the bowl felt deliciously warm. I lifted it up to my face and breathed it in.

"It's nothin'," I said with a shrug. "A few scratches is all."

"Nothin'?" protested Mrs. Redmond. "Yer soaked through, Charlie. Get on 'ome and find some dry clothes. Ya'll catch yer death in that lot."

I had no argument there. I was freezing.

"Thanks, Mrs. Redmond. I'll remember ta return yer bowl."

Careful not to spill any, I left the Redmonds on their porch and made my way through our front gate. Walking up the path, I spotted little Gracie Power, from number thirty-two, standing on the verandah holding something in her hands. Before I had a chance to say hello, Ma appeared at the door with Jack, who was busy feasting on her right breast.

"Hello, Gracie." Ma smiled. "What've ya got there, dear?"

For some reason, Gracie seemed to be having second thoughts about her visit. With tears in her eyes, she extended her arms and offered Ma the pot.

"Me ma sent me down with this," she sniffed. "It's only scraps . . . a few bones is all." Gracie blinked, sending the tears trickling down her dirty cheeks.

"What is it, dear?" asked Ma. "Is there somethin' upsettin' ya?"

"It's nothin', Mrs. Feehan."

"Nothin'? It must be somethin'. Yer cryin', child."

Gracie withdrew the pot and hugged it to her chest.

"It's not fair, that's all."

"What's not fair?"

"You lot ain't fair." She looked cross now. "Them scraps were fer me dog. Yer've no right ta be takin' 'em."

Suddenly the tenderness disappeared from Ma's face.

"Take 'em scraps back 'ome, Gracie," she snapped. "You give 'em ta ya dog. And while ya doin' it, you tell ya ma from me that she needn't be sendin' leftovers down. Scraps, indeed! Is it dogs she thinks we are?"

As Gracie scurried off, Ma caught sight of me, then took a step back.

"Good Lord, Charlie!" she shrieked. "Look at the state of ya."

The sudden noise startled Jack, who gave up the breast and began howling.

"I'm awright, Ma," I lied. "It were an accident in the schoolyard. . . . Here, Mrs. Redmond has sent some broth fer Jack."

"God bless her. Put it on the table, Charlie, and get outta them wet clothes."

Although our house was cold, I was thankful to be finally out of the rain. Before hobbling off to my room, I placed the bowl carefully on the table and found a dry towel in the cupboard.

First off were my boots. I pulled my feet free, then removed the small bundles of bloody newspaper and tossed them to a corner of the room. Next came my pants. Gingerly I slid them down over my bloody knees and dropped them onto the floor. I dabbed at my wounds with the towel, cleaning off bits of dirt until the towel was stained red. I removed the rest of my clothes and changed into a dry set. Having licked my wounds, I pulled an envelope, given to me by Squizzy himself, from my coat pocket, then rejoined Ma, who was spooning mouthfuls of warm broth into a delighted Jack.

"I've somethin' fer ya, Ma," I said, holding the envelope aloft. "It's a letter from Squizzy Taylor."

"A letter?" Ma smirked. "From Squizzy Taylor? What, and I s'pose yer've one from the Queen of England as well, 'ave ya?"

Excited, I dropped the envelope onto the table and sat down opposite her.

"Here, look fer yerself," I said. "It's yer name on it."

"'Mrs. Feehan,'" she read. "That's me, awright."

With her free hand, Ma opened the envelope and unfolded the letter.

"'Dear Mrs. Feehan,'" she began. "'It is with great pleasure that I write to you with what will, I am sure, prove to be a most convenient proposition.

"'First of all, you would do well to ignore the lies and accusations penned by some of this city's so-called journalists, for many among them have the morals of a common sewer rat. Just the other night, in fact, in a darkened alley, I did see with my own eyes one such rodent disappear into a drain with a typewriter tucked under his arm.

"'But let me assure you, a rogue I am not, nor a common criminal. I am a businessman, plain and simple.'"

For a brief moment, Ma raised her eyes from the ink and laughed.

"A businessman? Did ya 'ear that, Charlie? He calls 'imself a businessman?"

"Ma! Will ya just read the letter!"

Shaking her head, she scrolled a finger down the page, muttering the word as she went. "Businessman . . . businessman . . . businessman . . ." Halfway down, she found her place.

"'Ere we go. . . . 'And, as luck would have it,'" she continued, "'there has come a need to fill a position under my employ. This, missus, brings me to the proposition at hand.

"'I have in mind your Charlie boy for the position of runner. Such turn of foot, I have never seen in someone so young. I am told he also has a quick mind and a head for figures, which surely is a credit to your good self.

"'I am fully aware of your situation, what with your husband passing from the cough, and I mean no disrespect, but these are difficult times. Would not the winter months pass easier with an extra shilling or two in your purse?

"'I look forward to your reply. Yours respectfully, Leslie John Taylor, Esq.'"

When she was done reading, Ma pushed the letter across the table, then scooped another spoonful of broth into Jack's mouth.

"Well?" I asked.

"I can't allow it, Charlie."

I was shocked.

"Did ya not understand it, Ma? Read it again. Mr. Taylor wants me fer 'is runner. It's a paid job an' all."

"I know very well what it is, Charlie, and I'll not 'ave any son a mine keepin' company with criminals. Yer poor father'd be turnin' in 'is grave, God bless 'im. You'll stay at school and finish the year like 'e wanted."

"And what 'appens when the money runs out, Ma? What then?"

"Then ya'll find somethin' respectable ta do."

"Respectable? What, like stickin' labels on jam tins at Rosella's? Ma, this is a chance to earn some real coin. We're gunna be skint before long. Think about Jack."

At the mention of his name, her eyes shifted to him. He sat on her knee, dribbling, his wide eyes pleading for more broth. Again I looked at her face and saw a tear roll down her cheek.

"Think 'bout it, Ma. Ya 'aven't left the 'ouse since Pa died. Ya could start visitin' the neighbors again, like ya used ta. Remember that? I've done me sums, Ma, and I'd be earnin' twice as much as I would at Rosella's, maybe more. I'm fifteen, Ma."

"Charlie, I—"

"We could stop takin' 'andouts and leftovers . . . we could start livin' again, Ma, really livin'."

With her free hand, she picked up a bib from her lap and wiped her face dry.

"You tell ya Mr. Taylor ta find another boy," she sniffed. "We'll manage."

"But, Ma—"

"That's the end a it, Charlie. I'll not 'ear another word."

That night in my sleep, I dreamt of a house with pink walls.

In the main room, under the picture rails, a line of pretty white roses made a border around each of the walls. All three of us were there, Ma, Jack, and me, sitting in front of a crackling fire. Beside the hearth, stacked neatly in rows, was a pile of wood so high it reached the top of the mantelpiece. We sat smiling, faces aglow, dunking bits of bread into steaming soup. There was pudding, too. I could smell it, baking in the oven.

Next morning, it was the cold that woke me early. When I opened my eyes, the pink walls in my dream had turned a moldy gray and black. I curled up into a ball and began looking for objects in the patchy plaster to my right. It was like looking

at clouds. I could see things in that wall—a man smoking a pipe. Or was it a dragon breathing fire?

Whatever it was, I made a promise to myself, right then and there. One day I would live in a house with pink walls.

I dressed quickly and made my way down the hall. Halfway along I snuck a look into Ma's bedroom and saw her asleep in the bed. She looked so small, balled up under the blankets. So alone. For four days Ma and I had sat on that same bed and watched the Spanish flu eat my father up. I knew he would die, for the stench of death hung thick in the air. It was a sickly sweet smell, so strong you could taste it through the masks we were forced to wear. I hated those masks. Sometimes, when Ma left the room, I'd pull mine down for a few minutes and force myself to smile. I couldn't bear to touch him, like she did. It wasn't that I was afraid of catching something. It was his skin. It was so cold. But I had to be strong—for him.

It was quick, my father's death. I had little time to prepare for the end. As soon as he took his last breath, Ma and I were forced to think of the future. Even in death, the poor were denied the luxury of grieving. There just wasn't time.

On the twenty-sixth of February, at 11:20 a.m., when the undertakers came to wheel my father's lifeless body out to the hearse, it was as if they took my childhood with them. Like the other boys, I still wore knickerbockers in the schoolyard. I played queenie and marbles, too. But once the lessons were over, I returned home and stepped into the long pants of adulthood. I tell you, I got so confused sometimes, I didn't know who it was I was supposed to be.

In the kitchen, I cut a slice of bread and spread a layer of jam sparingly across the top. Things had changed since my

father died, especially Saturday mornings. I headed out the back door and spotted Harriet, our pathetic excuse for a duck, floating on the makeshift pond. For the record, Harriet was Ma's idea. We'd gone halves with the Redmonds on the understanding that any eggs laid would be split between the households. Three weeks she'd been here and in that time, nothing that had escaped from Harriet's hole was fit for eating. I'd tried everything. I gathered sewerage in buckets and built her the smelliest dam in Richmond. I shared my bread and talked to her in soothing tones. But still she continued to peck at my boots. On one occasion she charged at me so aggressively I had to retreat behind the kitchen door. If Harriet's attitude did not improve in the next few weeks, I, as her keeper, would be making a recommendation to her owners—pluck and bake.

Someone stirred behind me.

"Mornin', Harriet," said the voice.

It was Ma.

"What 'bout me?" I asked.

"Mornin', Charlie. Yer not upsettin' 'er, are ya?"

"Me? It's 'er is the nasty one."

Slowly, Ma took a few steps forward and opened her hand. Inside was a piece of bread.

"Careful, Ma," I warned. "She's a mind of 'er own."

With a gentle peck, Harriet took the bread from Ma's hand and in return received a pat on the head. Then, on my father's grave I do swear, that bird winked at me before waddling off.

Had there been time, I would have snuck up on Harriet right then and strangled her, but instead I made my way to the side of the house.

"I'll see ya later, Ma," I shouted.

"Awright, Charlie."

I grabbed the handle of my homemade trolley, steered it out into the street, and headed toward Fitzroy.

Before he died, my father had summoned friends to his bedside and called up favors. One of those friends was Gordon Peacock, a stocky man who worked at Stone's Timber Yard in Fitzroy. It was agreed that every Saturday morning, in return for raking the yard, I would be allowed to gather up bits of wood to take home. Nothing big, mind you, only splinters and pieces of fallen bark.

After a long walk, I arrived at the corner of Napier and Condell streets, where the Berger Paint sign covered the yard's fence.

PAINTS AND VARNISH, it said. KEEP ON KEEPING ON!

I steered my trolley through the gate and pulled up at the foreman's hut. Inside, Mr. Peacock was applying the finishing touches to a roll-your-own. He slid his tongue across the cigarette paper and smiled.

"Mornin', Charlie," he said. "There's a bit ta do today. How 'bout ya get stuck into it so we can shut up before the footy starts."

"Righto, Mr. Peacock. I'll make a start."

I stepped into the smoky hut and found the rake resting in the corner. On my way out, Mr. Peacock spat a stray flake of tobacco from the tip of his tongue.

"And 'ow's yer ma, Charlie?" he asked.

"She's okay."

"I'm glad ta 'ear it. She's a good woman, yer ma. Why don't ya tell 'er I'll call tomorra? Is there anythin' ya need?"

As you can imagine, there was plenty. I was about to reel

off a list, but something rose in my throat and stopped me. Pride, I think it was.

"No, thanks," I replied. "We're doin' fine."

That morning I spent two hours in the yard—one of them raking and the other searching for wood. The secret, albeit a little underhanded, was to throw in a couple of larger logs first, then cover them up with small stuff. By the end of it my trolley was loaded up, good and proper. To keep the wood dry on my long journey home, I secured a hessian cover over the top and said goodbye to Mr. Peacock.

I trod carefully home and kept a close eye on my bounty. Whenever I was forced to stop at an intersection, I stood astride the trolley to ward off prying eyes. So protective was I of that bulging load, it was as if I was steering the crown jewels through the streets of Melbourne.

Once I was home, Ma and I inspected the load.

"How'd ya go, Charlie?" she asked.

"Nothin' much, Ma," I lied. "A few splinters is all."

No matter how big the load, I could never resist playing games with her like that. I did it to see her smile. She was beautiful when she smiled.

I waited till she turned, then scooped off the splinters with my bare hands.

"Hang on a jiff," I said. "How'd those two logs get in there?"

In a flash, Ma was beside me, smiling, and for a few seconds I felt like the luckiest boy alive.

CHAPTER FOUR

I had little to do that afternoon, so I occupied myself spying on Harriet from the kitchen window. You learnt quickly how to survive in the slums. You learnt how to read people. It was in their walk, their clothes, and their eyes. Especially the eyes. Reading people was an art all right, but I tell you, this waddling ball of feathers had me stumped.

I propped myself on a chair, and soon enough a pattern emerged in Harriet's behavior. Eat, shit, swim—standard behavior for a duck. Harriet, like my brother, Jack, was fond of slugs. In the warmer months, before we'd purchased Harriet, I would take Jack out back and let him crawl around the yard. One day I let him loose, then left to get myself a chair. I'd only been gone a few seconds, but when I returned I saw him pick up a slug and pop it into his mouth.

Harriet was on the move. To avoid her seeing me, I dipped my head as she waddled toward the window, quacking excitedly. She pounced on a slug, picked it up with her beak, then shook her head to help it down her throat. Satisfied, she moved closer until she was underneath my window. I'd lost sight of her now. Afraid I might miss something, I raised myself up slowly until I could see her. Surely my eyes were playing tricks? There she was, standing before me, looking up into my eyes. Then, with God as my only witness, I swear, that duck had the nerve to smile.

With a supply of wood on hand, Saturday night was the highlight of our week, and after the incident with Harriet I was in need of some cheering up. As far as I knew, slugs preferred the outdoors, so I left Jack on the living room floor and joined Ma in the kitchen.

"Rabbit stew, is it, Ma?"

"It is, Charlie," she said. "I'm nearly ready fer ya. Why don't ya start stokin' the oven?"

Already my mouth was watering. I loved Ma's stews. Even though the pickings were slim, she had this knack of making things taste wonderful. I once heard someone say, "Ya can't make strawberry jam outta pig shit." I can't remember who it was that said it, but I can tell you, they had never sat down with the Feehans for dinner.

I loaded the oven with kindling and lit it. I was an expert with fires; my father had taught me well. Slowly, I placed larger pieces on top in a pyramid pattern, careful not to smother the flames, and before long it was ready for the pot.

As Ma loaded it in, I fetched Jack and, like every Saturday night, the three of us sat in front of the stove, happy and warm. Outside I heard Harriet quack-quacking, and I smiled.

"Yer've a smile on yer face, Charlie," said Ma. "I'll give ya a penny fer yer thoughts."

"I was just thinkin' 'bout Christmas dinner," I replied.

"Yer gettin' a bit ahead a yerself, ain't ya? . . . Awright, then, what d'ya fancy this year?"

"I'm thinkin' roast duck."

. . .

Rabbit stew was not the only highlight on a Saturday night. Saturday night was also bath night.

I filled the copper with buckets of water. Then, underneath it, I arranged the wood as before, pyramid-style, and lit it. Again, the three of us positioned ourselves around the kitchen stove, Ma and I rubbing our hands up close. This was our time. While we waited for the copper to boil, we talked. I dared not mention Squizzy's name to her, for I knew that anything I said would fall on deaf ears. It was pointless, anyway; on that score my mind was already made up. On Monday morning, as agreed, I would be fronting up for work, with or without my ma's consent.

From the copper, I relayed buckets of warm water to the bath. The water was never really hot. We were always mindful of saving some wood for the weekday cooking. So, even to fill the bathtub halfway, the going was slow. Still, you can imagine how excited we were. There was nothing on earth like sinking into a warm tub.

Jack was first, then Ma, then me.

Although the water was at its worst, I was happy enough to be last because Ma always insisted that I keep a little hot water in the copper to add to the bath before I dived in.

Finally my turn came. I stripped off, then carefully lowered myself into the tub, gasping each time the soapy water found my wounds.

Feet.

Knees.

Hands.

When the pain subsided, I sat back and let the soothing begin. I closed my eyes and slid a hand down to massage an ache on my right thigh. I was proud of my legs. Before the running, they'd been nothing more than two slender sticks. Chicken legs, my father had called them. But now with the miles in them, they were steely and strong. They were runner's legs—legs that would one day carry me out of the slums for good.

CHAPTER FIVE

After lunch the next day, I answered a knock on our front door. Mr. Peacock stood before me with a newspaper parcel tucked under his arm. His visit had completely slipped my mind.

"Afternoon, young Charlie."

"Afternoon, Mr. Peacock," I replied. "Would ya mind waitin' 'alf a jiff? I'll go and get Ma."

I raced into the kitchen and found Ma with her hands in the sink.

"There's somethin' I forgot ta tell ya, Ma," I confessed sheepishly.

"What is it, Charlie?"

"We've a visitor comin' over today."

"A visitor? I'm not acceptin' visitors no more."

"It's Mr. Peacock, Ma."

"Mr. Peacock? And when should we be expectin' 'im?"

"Er . . . 'e's 'ere, right now."

"What d'ya mean, 'e's 'ere?"

"I've left 'im at the front door."

If there was one thing that Ma prided herself on, it was her house. It was a dive for sure, but although people seldom came to visit anymore, she always made sure it was at its best.

"Good Lord, Charlie," she barked. "What are ya thinkin'? The place is a mess."

In a mad rush she tore off her apron and fiddled with her hair. Personally, I don't know why she was bothering. Mr. Peacock was an old friend. She fixed her dress before stepping into the hallway.

"Mr. Peacock . . . ya'll 'ave ta excuse Charlie, 'e's swallowed 'is manners with 'is dinner. Do come in outta the cold."

Smiling, Mr. Peacock removed his hat, then followed Ma inside. In the living room, he handed her the parcel and took a seat. It was my father's seat.

"I 'ope yer young'un likes chicken."

Ma blushed. "Chicken? Mr. Peacock, ya shouldn't 'ave."

Having no family of his own to speak of, Mr. Peacock had been a regular visitor to our house. Still, seeing him in my father's chair made me feel uneasy.

Overall, Mr. Peacock was a plain-looking man. The corners of his mouth were turned downward, making it look as though he'd been cursed with a permanent scowl. But there was a whiff of cologne about him today, and his appearance suggested he'd gone to some amount of trouble before stepping out. Never before had I seen him looking so smart. Except for a disobedient lock on the crown of his head, his hair was styled flat with a healthy serve of Brylcreem. Underneath a gray suit and matching vest, he wore a collarless white shirt, buttoned to the throat. And, for the first time, instead of boots he wore shoes, freshly polished.

I did not feel like talking, myself, so I sat for a while and listened. What little conversation passed between my ma and Mr. Peacock was awkward. Long silences filled the living room, punctuated by meaningless questions and answers. Everything had changed. In the past the link between them had been my father, but now with him gone they were like two strangers speaking for the first time.

He'd been a talker, my father, a chewer of ears. Whenever there was company around, he'd been at his best. So then, it may come as little surprise when I say that it was times like these that I missed my father most. I wanted him back. Not for them, but for me.

It got so that I felt I would suffocate in that tiny room. I was about to excuse myself when another knock sounded on the door.

Nostrils!

Leaping from my seat, I scampered up the hallway and answered the door. Behind it I found Nostrils emptying both barrels into a handkerchief. Had I known him better, I would have hugged him.

"Ma, this 'ere is Norman," I announced at the living room door.

She turned, thankful for the interruption.

Quickly I grabbed Nostrils' sleeve as he tried to enter the room.

"Hello, Norman," said Ma. "It's a pleasure. . . . I don't s'pose yer've met Mr. Peacock?"

"Can't say I 'ave, Mrs. Feehan. Good afternoon, Mr. Peacock."

After the formalities, Nostrils stood next to me and waited for my lead. We nodded politely, then bade farewell.

In the kitchen I lit some wood under the kettle, then pointed back to the living room.

"They were doin' me 'ead in before ya came," I explained. Poor Nostrils looked confused.

"Ya could a warned me, Charlie," he said. "At first I thought it was yer old man sittin' there."

"Who, 'im? Yer've got ta be kiddin'. Listen, d'ya want a cuppa?"

"Yeah, why not."

As I set up two cups, Nostrils shuffled to the window and looked outside.

"Yer keepin' a duck, I see?"

"It's Harriet." I scowled. "The bloody thing's playin' me fer a right mug. I've done me best ta keep her happy, but she refuses ta give us an egg. D'ya know anythin' about 'em?"

"As a matter a fact, I do, Charlie. And I think I can see yer problem from 'ere."

"Ya can? It's the dam, ain't it?"

"The dam looks fine, Charlie. Real invitin'. In fact, had I brought me togs with me, I'd be up fer a dip meself."

"Well, what is it, then?"

"It's Harriet," explained Nostrils. "I think ya ought'a change its name."

"What d'ya mean?"

"That there's no Harriet, Charlie."

"It ain't?"

"Nah. It's Harry."

After the cup of tea, Nostrils and I cleared out with the footy and headed to Barkly Gardens, in South Richmond. On the way we talked about many things, even my father. Besides my ma, I hadn't spoken to anyone about his death. Not properly, anyway. It had been two and a half months since they carried him away, and still I could not bring myself to say the word *dead*—it seemed so final, and I was not yet ready to let him go. But with Nostrils, it was different. He never pushed it, like other people. He just listened.

In the summer months, Barkly Gardens was the place to be. On a Sunday, families arrived early with picnic blankets to stake a claim on a piece of grass. They came for the band recitals that took place in the rotunda in the center of the gardens. But as it grew colder, the crowds began to thin.

Approaching the gardens, I booted the footy across the grass. I'd planned for a spiraling torpedo, but my foot caught it awkwardly, sending it off at a right angle in a flat mongrel punt.

"'Struth!"

"I see I'm gunna afta teach ya a couple a things," said Nostrils, smirking. "Ya'd be lucky ta get a game with Carlton, kickin' like that."

Suddenly Nostrils took off, plowing across the wet grass in search of the pigskin. He looked back and flashed me a crazy smile.

"Come on, Charlie," he roared. "I reckon ya was lucky the other day. Ain't no eggs ta think 'bout this time."

Although he had a start, I bounded after him. We reached the footy neck and neck, but it was Nostrils who wanted it more. With eyes only for the ball, he dived on top of it and slid across the grass.

"Whahoooooo!"

After showering himself in glory, Nostrils suggested we position ourselves for a kick.

"Who d'ya wanna be?" he asked.

Quickly I ran through the Richmond players I knew.

"I'll be Barney Herbert," I replied.

"Ya can't be Barney Herbert, he's a ruckman. Yer've gotta be someone scrawny, like yerself."

"Awright. I'll be Dave Moffatt, then."

Nostrils nodded his approval.

"Righto," he said. "And I'll be Vic Thorp, fullback."

For the next half an hour, Nostrils and I were Dave Moffatt and Vic Thorp. I did my best to be flashy. I scooped up the ball one-handed and dodged and weaved around imaginary opponents. Whenever I slipped, I heard the crowd cheering, willing me on. Through the center I sped, brushing tackles aside. One bounce. Two bounces. What a run! At the center half forward position I took a third bounce and unleashed a booming right foot. The ball sailed through the goals. Siren! I'd just won Richmond the flag.

I was pathetic, really. No match at all for Nostrils at the other end. Even I could see that. He was taller than me by a good three inches, and thicker-set. In full flight, good players have a certain grace about them, and Nostrils was no exception. He had balance and style galore. And skill! He had it in bucketloads. Drop punt. Torpedo. Drop kick. He reeled them off as easy as blowing his nose.

I stood ready at the other end as Nostrils lined one up. He dropped the ball onto his boot so sweetly that it sailed over my head and headed for the rotunda. I'd done a fair amount of chasing already, so I jogged after it at an easy pace. I was almost there when I spotted a group of boys coming down the rotunda steps.

One of them spoke.

"Feehan!"

It was Barlow.

Standing some twelve yards away, I quickly sized up my options. There were six of them and one of me—unbackable odds in anyone's book. Not even Squizzy would be interested in a piece of that. My eyes got busy, shifting between the footy and the boys. At the head of the pack, Barlow made a move. He dismounted the steps and scooped up the footy.

"Look what we 'ave 'ere, lads." He smiled. "Charlie Feehan 'ere 'as kindly donated us a footy."

With his right fist he off-loaded a sizzling handball that caught one of his mates off guard. Then suddenly, something in his head clicked.

"Get 'im!" he yelled.

Not surprisingly, I was ready for them. I jumped out of the blocks and ran. Speeding across the wet grass, I thought about Barlow's handball. Only this time my head was the footy.

Up ahead, Nostrils was ambling toward me, confused. My arms were busy pumping the air, so I warned him the only way I could.

I screamed, "Run!"

The change on Nostrils' face told me he'd spotted Barlow—a good enough reason to get going right then and there. Instead, Nostrils did something I'll never forget.

He waited.

Fortunately, he had the good sense to point himself in the right direction, so when I drew near he took off beside me.

Then together, we ran for our lives.

I don't know about Nostrils, but I can tell you, it felt as if someone had stuck a firecracker down the seat of my pants.

When we left the wetness of the grass, both of us lengthened our stride. I could sense that we'd widened the gap on Barlow and his mates, so I snuck a look back. I was right. Already two of them were down, and the others appeared to be slowing. In their haste for blood they'd forgotten about the conditions underfoot. We were away.

It was only when we crossed the railway track near Church Street that Nostrils and I slowed to a walk.

"Can ya believe it, Nostrils?" I puffed. "That waster pinched me footy."

"Don't worry, Charlie. I've a feelin' we'll be seein' 'im again. Maybe if yer real polite 'e'll give it back. Only remind me not to be standin' next ta yer when ya ask."

CHAPTER SIX

Monday morning I stirred early. I dressed in my cleanest clothes, then dug out the box of newspapers from under my bed. By now I'd become an expert. I slid on my boots, then began filling the holes.

Apart from the fact that I would be running messages, I'd been told little about my new job. I was to report to the Darlington Parade house at nine o'clock. That was all.

With my shoes packed tight, I headed to the kitchen and fixed myself some porridge. Ma joined me with Jack.

"That'll get ya learnin'." She smiled, pointing to the oats.

As far as Ma was concerned, Monday morning had started like any other. It was only I who knew it to be different. I was not proud to be going behind her back like this, and under normal circumstances I would have obeyed her wishes without question. But our circumstances were far from normal now. This was our chance at something better, and I would not let it slip for anyone. Not even my own ma.

After a leisurely walk, I knocked on the Darlington Parade door with five minutes to spare. A woman, the same one who'd carried the tray of eggs on race day, opened the door and smiled. She smelt like lavender.

"Ya must be Charlie?" she asked.

"I am, miss."

"Me name's Dolly, Charlie. Ya did well the other day. Come on through."

I followed Dolly down the darkened hall and into the living room.

"Take a seat, Charlie," she said. "Squizzy's bought ya somethin'."

On a table next to the divan, Dolly retrieved a parcel and sat down next to me. She sat so close I could smell the tea on her breath.

"When I say 'e bought 'em, 'e did. But it was me what chose 'em."

Slowly she opened the lid and removed a pair of shiny black boots.

"Well, Charlie, what d'ya reckon? They're leather."

I sat wide-eyed, unable to speak.

She smiled. "I took a punt on the size. I 'ope they fit."

Although I was excited, nothing came from my mouth.

"Come on, then, let's try 'em on."

Next thing I knew, Dolly was bent down untying the laces on my father's boots.

"I was gunna get the brown, but I thought the dirt'd show up less on the black."

As I bent down to help her, my head hit hers.

"Sorry," I said.

"It's awright, Charlie, no need ta be shy. What say we get rid a these stinkin' things?"

Standing with her arms fully stretched, she held the boots away from her nose as if she was handling something unspeakable. Suddenly I found my voice.

"I might keep 'em if ya don't mind, Dolly."

"What, these?" she asked. "I've a good mind ta go out the back and bury 'em."

"They were me father's," I said softly.

Slowly Dolly sat down beside me and placed a gentle hand on my shoulder. Her blue eyes were close to tears.

"Oh, Charlie. I'm sorry. I can be a right cow sometimes. 'Ere, how about I put 'em back in this nice box?"

"Thanks."

Off to my right, Squizzy appeared through the doorway.

"Hello, then," he chortled. "What's goin' on 'ere? Yer not tryin' ta steal me girl, are ya, Charlie?"

I was shocked.

"Mr. Taylor, I swear, I never—"

"Charlie, it's awright," he laughed. "I'm messin'. How are the boots?"

Dolly waved him off, annoyed.

"Hang on ta yer trousers, Squiz," she said. "We 'aven't tried 'em on yet."

With my father's boots tucked safely in the box, Dolly slid the new pair onto my feet. I tell you, I'd never felt anything so smooth in all my life. She tied the laces, then gave my feet a playful squeeze.

"Go on, then, Charlie." She smiled. "'Ave a walk."

Slowly I rose to my feet and stepped a lap around the room.

"Well?" asked Dolly, still kneeling.

"They're perfect," I said.

"Yer sure now? We can exchange 'em if they don't fit."

"They fit fine, Dolly. Thanks."

Behind me I heard Squizzy clap.

"Good," he said. "'Cause I got a job fer ya, Charlie. Come on, shake a leg."

Before I made to leave, Dolly threw me a wink.

I followed Squizzy down the hall, stepping across floor-boards as if I was walking on air. At the end of the house I entered a large room with piles of paper scattered across the floor. Boxes, some of them open, lined the walls, and a wooden table stood heavy, center place.

"I've not 'eard from yer ma, Charlie," said Squizzy. "D'ya have a letter fer me?"

"I'm afraid I don't, Mr. Taylor," I said nervously. "It's some-thin' I've been meanin' ta talk ta ya about."

Squizzy took a seat behind the table and indicated with his hand that I should sit.

"She's not agreed ta me runnin' fer ya. She thinks I'm at school."

"Is that so? And what school is it yer supposed ta be attendin'?"

"Saint Ignatius, sir."

Squizzy's chair creaked as he eased back into it. He sat for a while, thinking.

"I'm not normally one ta go against the wishes of a mother, Charlie. But I'm in desperate need of a lad like yerself. Who's yer teacher at Saint Ignatius?"

"It's Mrs. Nagle, sir."

On a piece of paper, Squizzy wrote her name.

"Mrs. Nagle, eh? Might be worth payin' 'er a visit. And d'ya 'ave report cards sent 'ome, Charlie?"

"We do, Mr. Taylor."

"And what is it yer good at? Sums?"

"Yeah, sums is me best. I'm not much good at spellin', though."

"Don't ya worry 'bout it, Charlie. I'll fix it with Mrs. Nagle . . . get 'er ta bump yer grades up, while we're at it. Just quietly, lad, I think ya'll find yer spellin' is about ta improve."

"Really?" I was shocked. "Ya mean I don't 'ave ta go ta school no more?"

"That's right, Charlie. Yer no good ta me with yer 'ead stuck in a book all day. Right, 'ere's the job fer ya."

CHAPTER SEVEN

During my first week under Squizzy's employ, I was surprised how few errands I ran. When I did, it was mainly small stuff. Maybe he was testing me.

I picked up creams and lotions for Dolly at Madame Ghurka's at the Eastern Market in Bourke Street, and on one occasion Squizzy entrusted me with a sum of money to fetch a silver brooch he'd had engraved.

None of the errands was urgent, so I was able to run at a leisurely pace, and as I pounded the pavement I caught myself, more than once, looking down at my shiny new boots.

In between jobs, rather than sit around lazing, I offered to wash Squizzy's car. I washed it so clean I could see myself in it. After he'd inspected it, Squizzy told me that I had more initiative than most of the men who worked for him. I liked that.

Friday afternoon came around quick. When I'd finished the day's work, I made my way to the laundry at the back of the house, as I did every afternoon. In a corner I found the shoe box. It nearly broke my heart to do it, but I sat down on the concrete floor, undid the laces on my new boots, and slid them off. I then replaced them with my father's pair. As soon as my feet were inside them, I couldn't wait for Monday.

Back inside the house, I said goodbye to Dolly, then found Squizzy in his chair behind the table.

"Ya did well this week, Charlie," he said, opening a drawer beside him. He pulled out an envelope and slid it across the table. "I'm thinkin' ya'll be well pleased with what's inside."

Slowly I reached a trembling hand across the table and picked it up.

"Thanks, Mr. Taylor. When will ya be wantin' me next?"

"There's somethin' just come up, as a matter a fact. Tomorra night. It's a job fer two."

Suddenly a face flashed before my eyes. It was Nostrils.

"I know of someone, Mr. Taylor," I said. "Norman Heath. Ya might remember 'im from race day. He was the blue runner."

"The lad with the big nose, was 'e?"

"That's 'im."

"Awright, Charlie. Ya bring 'im along. Be 'ere at eight o'clock."

With my first wages in my hand, I walked out the front door and pushed through the gate. My whole body shook. For a while I could not even look at the envelope for fear it was all a dream. Then, some way up the street, I stopped. Carefully I tore open the flap and pulled out a pound note. I scrunched my fingers around it tight, then steadied myself by grabbing hold of a nearby fence with my free hand.

With the rain on my face, I lifted my fist to the heavens and threw my father a wink.

"Giddyup!"

Next morning, the first thing I heard was Jack. I rolled onto my side and opened my eyes. On the moldy wall opposite I saw a dog with three legs. It was a small dog, a terrier like the one Mr. and Mrs. Redmond owned.

For a while I did not move. I lay there thinking about the day ahead. There was the wood run, of course, and after that, maybe a bit of rabbiting in the afternoon. Then . . .

Suddenly I bolted upright in bed. I swung my legs out from under the blankets and dived onto the floor. In seconds my hand was jammed down the side of the box of newspapers under my bed.

The envelope!

Frantically my fingers began searching. Last night I'd thought it a clever idea to hide the envelope in a box of papers, but now I wasn't so sure. I panicked. Each time I thought I had it, I came up with bits of torn newsprint. Finally I found it near the bottom. I sat back against the bed and held the pound note in my hand.

It was real. And it was mine.

Later that morning, on arriving at Stone's Timber Yard, I found Mr. Peacock to be strangely offhand. As always, I parked my trolley near the foreman's hut and poked my head inside.

"Good mornin', Mr. Peacock," I chirped.

I waited for a reply, but he kept his eyes on the paper in front of him and said nothing.

"I'll just fetch the rake and get started, then, shall I?"

"There's no wood fer ya today," he said.

"No wood?" I asked. "I think yer mistaken, Mr. Peacock. I seen some scattered about the yard on me way in."

Suddenly Mr. Peacock looked up and spoke to me with a loud voice.

"Did ya not 'ear me?" he spat. "There's no wood fer ya

today. Go 'ome and tell yer ma. And tell 'er I'll be callin'
tomorra."

Slowly I backed out of the hut and started for home with
an empty trolley. I was stunned. Never before had Mr. Peacock
spoken to me like that, and never before had he refused me a
load of wood. On the long walk home I turned things over and
over in my head. I had been there when the agreement was
made, when Mr. Peacock shook hands with my father. I had
heard him promise. I had seen him.

When I reached home, I was none the wiser. Instead of
leading my trolley through the back door, I left it down the side
and trudged into the house. Ma saw me coming.

"And 'ow'd ya get on today, Charlie?" she asked.

"There's no wood today, Ma."

"No wood? What on earth are ya talkin' 'bout?"

"It's like I said, there's no wood. Mr. Peacock told me ta tell
ya. He'll be callin' tomorra."

Slowly Ma turned her face from me and found a seat at the
kitchen table. I followed until I was standing before her. She
was crying.

"What is it, Ma? What's 'appened?"

"It's nothin', Charlie."

"I'm sorry 'bout the wood, Ma."

"It's not yer fault, luv."

"What'll we do, then?"

With her sleeve, she wiped away some tears. Then she
smiled at me—the saddest smile I'd ever seen.

"Don't ya worry," she said. "I know what ta do."

CHAPTER EIGHT

When I called at Nostrils' house in Mary Street that Saturday afternoon, the two of us were fit to burst. Both of us had news.

"Come on in, Charlie," he said. "There's somethin' I've got ta tell ya."

I tied up the Redmonds' terrier, Clarrie, to the front fence and followed him inside.

In the living room, his mother and father sat at the table, admiring a freshly baked sponge cake sitting on a plate in front of them.

"At last," said his father. "We meet the mysterious Charlie Feehan. Ya'll have a piece a cake with us, won't ya, Charlie?"

"I will, Mr. Heath," I said. "Thanks."

I took a seat next to Nostrils, and before long Mrs. Heath was back at the table with another plate.

"Go on, then, Norman." She smiled proudly. "I don't want Charlie 'ere thinkin' it's every day we 'ave sponge cake. Good Lord, before long we'll 'ave 'alf the neighborhood visitin'. Tell 'im before me 'eart packs it in."

Beside me Nostrils was playing with his fork.

"I've been picked ta play with the Richmond Hill team," he said with a grin. "They want me ta start trainin' on Wednesday."

My mouth opened, but nothing came. It was something that seemed to be happening a lot lately. Having seen Nostrils with a football in his hands, I had no reason to doubt him. Even so, I looked around the table for confirmation. Mr. and Mrs. Heath nodded excitedly.

"Richmond Hill?" I asked.

They nodded again.

"Crikey!"

With our bellies full of cake, Nostrils and I set off with Clarrie for Yarra Park. The three of us doubled back toward Cubitt Street, and where the train tracks veered into one, Clarrie flattened his ears and began pulling on the lead.

Rabbits.

Besides Billy Morgan's ferret, Clarrie was the best rabbiter in Richmond. Small only in stature, he was named, fittingly, after Clarrie Hall, the ferocious Richmond rover.

Pink noses twitched that little bit faster when Clarrie was let off the lead. He scurried around rabbit holes, chasing down anything that moved. At Yarra Park, when Clarrie came out to play, one thing was for certain—you never went home empty-handed.

Soon enough Clarrie emerged from the bush with a rabbit in his mouth. He trotted up to us, then sat at our feet, panting.

"Give it 'ere!" I commanded.

Carefully, I took the stunned rabbit from him, wrung its neck, and threw its lifeless body to the ground. Sensing the game was over, Clarrie licked his bloody jaw, then bolted off for more.

Since I'd met with Nostrils, the talk had been mostly about football. Now it was my turn.

"There's a job on tonight I'll be needin' a hand with," I said. "Ya interested?"

"Tonight?" asked Nostrils. "Too right I am."

"Beaut. Squizzy ain't told me much, but I reckon there'll be a quid or two in it fer ya. We're on at eight o'clock."

"Yeah, course. Count me in."

After a couple of hours, Clarrie's kill count totaled five. I gave a rabbit to Nostrils, tied the others by the legs, then slung them over my right shoulder.

"Rabbit stew," I said, wiping my hands. "Ya don't get much fresher than that."

Seeing as most nights I went out running, Ma paid little attention to my departure from the house that night. Just before eight, I met Nostrils at the corner of Swan and Church streets as planned.

Despite the rain, Nostrils was all smiles.

"Nice night fer it, eh, Charlie?"

"Could be worse," I replied.

Together we walked up Church Street, our coat collars standing at attention. Except for the company, there wasn't much to like about that cold and miserable night. Already my clothes were wet through.

"Don't s'pose the boss pays extra when it's rainin', does 'e?" panted Nostrils.

"I dunno. Why don't ya ask 'im and find out?"

Arriving at the Darlington Parade house, I knocked on the door and waited. Instead of Dolly, a gent I recognized from race day answered. One of the sheep, I think he was.

"Evenin'," I said. "Charlie Feehan and Norman Heath. We're 'ere fer Mr. Taylor."

Leaning against the doorway, the gent looked annoyed, as if we'd interrupted something.

"Squizzy and Dolly are attendin' the theater," he said, retreating into the house. "Come through—'e's left yer instructions back 'ere somewhere."

From the table in the study, the gent picked up a piece of paper and handed it to me. I didn't bother showing it to Nostrils, what with his memory the way it was. Instead, I kept it to myself.

It read:

Pickup—22 Goodwood Street, Richmond

Drop-off—12 Erin Street, Richmond

Satisfied he'd done his bit, the gent turned to leave.

"Hang on a jiff," I protested. "What is it that needs ta be done?"

Again the gent looked annoyed.

"Don't tell me ya never run the rabbit before," he snapped.

"Run the rabbit?" asked Nostrils.

"Flamin' 'eck, am I gunna 'afta 'old yer 'ands? You'll be doin' a liquor run. Written down's the pickup and the drop-off address. It's a piece a cake."

Despite the explanation, Nostrils and I stood together, unmoving.

"Is there somethin' else, ladies?" asked the gent.

"Nothin'," I said.

"Good. I'll ask ya ta be off, then."

This time we led ourselves out. At the door the gent stopped me and pulled me away from Nostrils.

"It's Charlie, ya said?"

"That's right," I replied.

"Listen, lad, I've been around the traps fer a while. D'ya want me advice?"

"Sure."

Over my shoulder the gent looked at Nostrils and broke into a smile.

"If the rain gets too 'eavy fer ya, why don't ya try standin' under 'is nose?"

At a brisk walking pace, Nostrils and I headed for the pickup address. For the residents of Richmond, only one person came to mind whenever Goodwood Street was mentioned. That person was Henry Stokes. Stokes was a self-proclaimed Good Samaritan—a man whose calling in life was to serve the good people of Richmond.

The truth?

Stokes was an SP bookmaker and sly grogger who'd done so well at his trade that he'd managed to build up a small fortune. As part of his tireless charity work, he ran Melbourne's biggest two-up school. And with hotels forced to close at six o'clock, Stokes supplied liquor after hours at highly inflated prices.

It was a far cry from the softly spoken Madame Ghurka with her creams and lotions. This was organized crime, and Nostrils and I were about to dip our toes in.

From Lennox Street we turned left into Goodwood.

"Ya never said nothin' about Goodwood Street," said Nostrils nervously.

"Ya never asked," I replied. "Anyway, ya never told me about Barlow, remember? I reckon that makes us even."

"Cripes, Charlie. Next ya'll be tellin' me we're goin' ta Stokes' place."

I tried to keep walking, but Nostrils grabbed hold of my arm.

"I hope ya know what yer doin', Charlie."

Pulling up, I turned and faced him.

"Listen, Nostrils, we're workin' fer Squizzy Taylor. Did ya think we'd be pickin' up liquor from an old boiler in slippers?"

"We're talkin' 'bout Henry Stokes, Charlie."

"Don't worry, Nostrils. All we gotta do is pick it up and deliver it. We'll be done in 'alf an 'our."

After a bit of lip biting, Nostrils relented.

"Awright, let's get it over with."

From my nightly runs along Goodwood Street I'd learnt that the entrance to the two-up school was down the side of the house. Nostrils followed closely behind until we were positioned in front of a heavy wooden door.

"Ya ready?" I asked.

Nostrils nodded.

I cannot say that I wasn't nervous, but for me there was something far more powerful at work. I was excited. I didn't want what other people wanted. I didn't want to be like Nostrils, sticking labels on tins of jam at Rosella's, or like my father, who'd busted his gut down on the wharf for years. I wanted something more than that. I wanted a piece of the action. It didn't have to be a huge helping, just a slice of it.

Enough to give Ma and Jack a better life.

I knocked.

In the door just above our heads a panel opened. Two eyes spoke to us.

"What?"

I lifted myself onto my toes and shouted.

"Mr. Taylor 'as sent us. We're 'ere fer the liquor run."

Behind the door a lock clicked open and in an instant a beefy bouncer appeared before me.

"Jaysus, lad, why don't ya tell the whole bloody neighborhood?"

Straightaway I picked him for a boxer. He had no neck to speak of, and his flattened nose suggested he'd copped more than his fair share of punishment in the ring. At the very least I was expecting a clip across the ear, but when he caught sight of Nostrils something in the tough man seemed to soften. I stepped aside and saw that the two of them were locked in a gaze, smiling. I think it was a nose thing.

"Sorry 'bout the din," said Nostrils. "Would ya be so kind as ta tell us where it is we pick up the grog?"

Hearing Nostrils speak, the bouncer relaxed and dropped his shoulders. Blow me down! He did have a neck—a good half inch at least.

"'Round the back, lads," he said. "There's a bell at the side of the door. Ask fer Jenkins. Oh, and keep it down, will ya?"

This time it was me who followed Nostrils. I drew next to him and punched him playfully on the arm.

"Nice work, Nostrils. Yer a natural at this caper."

At the rear door Nostrils stepped forward and gave the bell a ring. Not long after, an older man with a standard-type nose appeared in the doorway.

"Jenkins?" asked Nostrils.

"That's me."

"We're Squizzy Taylor's lads, sent fer the liquor."

"Come through, lads. I've been expectin' ya."

We followed Jenkins through the doorway and into a room packed with liquor. At a desk off to the right he shuffled through a pile of papers.

"'Ere it is," he said. "Let's see . . . two whisky, one gin, and a 'alf dozen bottles a beer. Must be some shindig."

Carefully Jenkins loaded the beer into an old cement bag, then fetched the whisky and gin.

"Is it far yer've gotta go?" he asked.

"Not far," I replied. "It's only up ta Erin Street."

Jenkins nodded.

"Yis can work it out between yerselves who takes what, but I suggest one of ya stick these two in yer coat pocket and the other carries the beer."

Nostrils took the whisky and gin, leaving me the beer. Not wanting to cause a scene, I carefully twisted the top of the bag and lifted it off the ground.

"Don't just stand there, Nostrils," I groaned. "Give us a hand, will ya?"

Outside, my legs reacted quickly to the weight over my shoulder. With Nostrils at my side, we plodded up Goodwood Street, then turned left into Lennox. It was time to have words with Nostrils.

"I 'ope yer not fergettin' who the apprentice is 'ere," I said. "If yer attitude don't improve, I'll be dockin' yer pay."

At Bridge Road, with only a few streets left to travel, Nostrils offered to take a turn lugging the bottles. Maybe if he'd made the suggestion earlier, I would have been more impressed. Even so, I was glad for the spell.

We continued up Lennox Street, then turned left into Erin, looking for the drop-off address.

Six . . . eight . . . ten . . . twelve.

Standing outside number twelve, Nostrils lowered the bottles to the ground and grimaced as he grabbed at his lower back.

"'Struth."

He was taking the piss, surely.

"I 'ope yer not overdoin' it, Nostrils," I said. "Is there anythin' I can get yer? A cup a tea, maybe?"

"I'll be right, thanks, Charlie. Just give us a minute."

Standing in front of the pretty white terrace house, I spotted movement out of the corner of my eye. I swung my head left and saw a copper waltzing up the street toward us.

"Quick, Nostrils, we got company."

In a flash, I grabbed the bottles and stepped over the low fence in front of me. Across the lawn, I headed to a thick bush and ducked in behind it. Luckily, Nostrils came with me. As soon as I sat, I knew it was a bad move. Directly above us was a window, and inside a light burned so bright, it had the two of us lit up like a nativity scene.

There was no time to move, so we dropped close to the ground, our heads only inches apart. Lying low, I leaned forward and found one of Nostrils' ears.

"Yer makin' one 'ell of a racket," I whispered.

"Sorry, but me nose is blocked."

"Why don't ya try breathin' through yer mouth, then?"

Between the branches the copper appeared at the front fence. He stopped and let his eyes wander around the front garden. For sure, we were gone. He seemed to be looking directly at us but showed no sign of having seen us. Then, slowly, he began to move off. Just to be sure, I waited a few minutes, then signaled to Nostrils I was going to check the street. At the front fence I looked left, then right. It was all clear.

Quickly Nostrils and I picked up the bottles and knocked on the front door.

A well-dressed gent with a neat mustache answered.

"We're 'ere with yer liquor, sir."

"Crikey, lads, you're covered in leaves," said the gent. "What 'ave you been up to?"

"We was nearly sprung by a copper out front," I explained.

"Is that so?" He smiled. "You needn't have been bothered with 'im, lads. He's one of mine."

I snuck a look at Nostrils and panicked.

"Ya mean yer a copper yerself?"

"I was a long time ago. I've been promoted since. Inspector, I am now. Did you bring the whisky and gin with you?"

"We did, sir."

I took the bottles from my coat pockets and handed them over. Before picking up the cement bag, the inspector found a shilling coin and flicked it to me.

"Good work, lads," he said, backing away from the door. "Oh, and give my regards to Squizzy, would you?"

Smiling, Nostrils and I walked out along the path and found the copper waiting for us at the front gate. Up close he looked none too pleased to be out in the rain.

"Nice night fer it, Constable," said Nostrils.

"Ain't nothin' nice about it. What's yer caper, you two?"

"We're just visitin'," I explained. "Business."

"Business?"

Slowly the penny dropped and the copper realized the

reason for our visit. I stood next to Nostrils, smiling confi-
dently, almost daring the copper to take it further.

Never before would I have had the nerve, but as he looked
into my eyes I held his gaze, and it was then that I realized what
it was I loved about working for Squizzy Taylor. It was more
than just the money. It was the power I loved as well.

CHAPTER NINE

Sunday morning I saw a strange woman in the mold on my bedroom wall. She had no face to speak of, so I made her Mrs. Nagle.

Suddenly she came to life.

Long division, Charlie Feehan. Open your book at page twelve.

Crikey! She was giving me sums!

After that, a succession of women appeared—Mrs. Hargraves at number seven, Madame Ghurka, Nostrils' mum . . . none of them in the least bit happy to be up there. The faces continued changing, faster and faster, then stopped with just one face.

It was Dolly—Squizzy's Dolly.

Get outta bed, ya lazy bugger, she said.

Then she was gone.

Reluctantly, I dragged myself from my warm bed and scooted up the hall. I found Ma sitting on a kitchen chair feeding Jack with a blanket wrapped around her shoulders. I'd slept in.

"How is 'e this mornin', Ma?" I asked.

"He's freezin' cold, Charlie, how d'ya expect 'e is?"

The icy reception shocked me. In all the times we'd gone without wood, I'd never known Ma to raise her voice at me.

"Are ya awright, Ma?"

She looked up and gave me that sad smile.

"I'm sorry, Charlie," she said softly. "I didn't mean ta snap. I'm not feelin' meself today."

"Shall I call next door and see if the Redmonds can spare some wood?"

"No. We can't keep scroungin' off the neighbors, Charlie. It ain't right."

"But Jack, 'e's freezin' cold, ya said?"

"Charlie, will ya stop!" She was screaming now. "I don't need ya remindin' me 'e's cold. Fer God's sake, will ya get outta me 'air."

Ever since Mr. Peacock's visit to our house last Sunday, I'd noticed a change in my mother's mood. Something was troubling her, I could sense it.

This time, the tone in her voice stung me. I'd never seen her so wild. Wounded, I took off down the hall, pushed through the front door, and ran.

It didn't matter where. All I wanted was to get away. Street after street, I kept running, driving her words from my head. After a good hour, I limped back up Cubitt Street, exhausted, until I was outside our house again. Next door, Mr. Redmond waved.

"'Struth, Charlie, ya look like ya run all the way ta Sydney and back. Ya wanna catch the train next time. Tell me, was it rainin' up there?"

"Not a drop, Mr. Redmond," I said. "In fact, it was so warm, I could a stopped fer a swim."

I stepped onto our porch and quietly opened the door, just in case Ma was napping in her bed. Once inside I breathed a familiar scent—a sickly perfume smell it was. Slowly I made my way down the hall and stopped in the kitchen door. At first I thought the room was empty, but then I saw them up against the sink. Mr. Peacock had his mouth on Ma's neck, moaning. I ducked in behind the door and watched as Ma let my father's friend kiss her. Then I realized something—the moaning sound I had heard wasn't Mr. Peacock at all. It was my ma, crying.

I could not bear to look. The very sight of them made my stomach churn. I turned my head and quietly headed to my room. At first I thought about running again, losing myself in the streets, but I hadn't the strength. Instead, I slipped under the blankets and folded the pillow tight around my ears.

That night I turned sixteen years old.

On Monday morning I could not bring myself to look at Ma. Sitting at the table, I felt uneasy. When I was forced to speak to her, I focused my eyes on Jack. One time, as I reached for the jam, she touched my arm and I jumped clean out of my chair.

Not yet three months my father had been gone—three lousy months.

She had no right to be wearing his ring anymore. I was ashamed.

Without so much as a goodbye, I rose from my chair and left the house.

I needed air.

Trudging up Cubitt Street, however, did nothing to lift my spirits. My father used to say that if you wanted to know about a place, all you had to do was walk down its streets. He was right.

The streets of Richmond were like the pages in a book. They told a story.

It was no fairy tale with rosy middles and happy endings. This story was full of hardship. Hand to mouth and day to day, that's how it was.

For those outsiders game enough to heed my father's advice, the first thing they noticed was the air. Industry boomed in Richmond. There were the tanneries, the breweries, the boiling-down works, the cork factory, the jam factory, and the tip. When the wind was blowing right, that lot got together and let loose with the foulest concoction of fumes you could ever imagine. Nostrils, with his keen nose, reckoned that on one particular day he detected seventeen different stenches in the air. And in all seriousness, I had no reason to doubt him.

Besides the factories, we also had the fishos and the rabbitos, who cleaned their wares on carts, then tossed the bloody remains into the gutters for the cats and dogs. These were the same gutters that children played in—a playground full of blood and guts, of horse manure, empty tins, and rats.

Over the next couple of weeks I threw myself into my work with such enthusiasm that Squizzy ran out of jobs for me. No matter what the job or how trivial it seemed, I ran every errand as if my life depended on it. Running was all I had now. At least no one could spoil that. Running belonged to me.

I ran during the day and I ran at night. In fact, I ran so much that I didn't bother changing into my father's old boots anymore. Ma and I both had our secrets now. At home I felt more like a tenant than a son. I avoided her as best I could, preferring to spend my time with Nostrils or Squizzy or Dolly. At least with them I didn't have to pretend.

One evening I returned home from a run, covered in sweat and feeling strong. I slipped through the front door and heard raised voices toward the back of the house. Jack was at it, too. Quickly I marched down the hall and found Mr. Peacock slurring foulmouthed obscenities at Ma, who he had trapped against the sideboard. Bits of shattered glass lay scattered across the kitchen floor. I smelt whisky.

"What the flamin' 'eck's goin' on?" I roared.

Hearing my voice, Ma stepped to the side with her arms up high, protecting her face.

"Charlie!"

When she tried to move past him, it was then that I saw what he'd done. He'd taken to her with his fists. Her lip was split open, and one of her eyes was swollen to the size of a cricket ball.

Mr. Peacock turned and saw me coming.

"Back off, lad," he spat. "It don't concern ya."

As I rushed forward, he jumped before me and hit me on the jaw with a right hook that sat me on the floor. Ma screamed. Full of rage, I lifted myself up and hurtled off down the hall to my bedroom. Under the bed, I found my cricket bat next to the box of papers and dragged it out. I was wild.

The voices seemed to be getting louder, so I ran back down the hall toward them. Halfway down, I could see him laying into her. I charged. At the doorway I decided against playing Mr. Peacock with a straight bat. I stormed into the kitchen and raised the willow, cross-bat style. I was nearly there when Mr. Peacock turned. He saw me all right. But he was too slow. I gripped the handle tight, cocked it over my shoulder, and brought the edge of the bat down hard across his skull. *Crack!*

Almost immediately his lights went out and his limp body dropped to the ground. Standing above him, I suddenly felt quite calm. Already a small trail of blood was snaking its way down onto his face. I watched it pool in his eye socket, then continue its journey over the bridge of his nose, finally dripping into a puddle of whisky on the floor.

"Holy Saint Francis," breathed Ma. "What 'ave ya done, Charlie?"

To be honest, I didn't know.

For a few moments, Ma and I stood there looking at his lifeless body, waiting for it to move. It didn't, so I gave his ribs a gentle nudge with the bat.

"Is 'e dead?" I asked.

"Good Lord, Charlie, 'ow should I know? Is it a doctor ya think I am? Come and 'elp me with some towels."

Soon Ma and I were bent down wrapping towels around Mr. Peacock's bloody skull.

"He don't look well, Ma," I said. "Is 'e still breathin'?"

Before she had time to answer, Mr. Peacock moved his arm.

"Quickly, Charlie, go and fetch Mr. Redmond from next door."

"But—"

"Go, Charlie! And take yerself off fer a while."

Halfway up Cubitt Street, after visiting the Redmonds, I turned and saw Mr. Redmond darting through our front gate in his dressing gown, and for the first time I understood the trouble I was in. It had never occurred to me, as I charged down the hallway, to aim for Mr. Peacock's legs. I'd wanted to hurt him. After all, a man with a belly full of liquor never gives you a second chance. You're best to drop him with your first shot.

But now, without my hackles up, I realized I'd gone too far. So instead of heading to Nostrils' house in Mary Street, as was my original plan, I ducked up Church Street and headed to Darlington Parade.

When I arrived at Squizzy's door, the panic had ahold of me so bad I could barely raise my hand to knock. I leaned my forehead on the wooden door and kicked at its base with my boot.

The outside light clicked on, and soon Squizzy appeared at the door, dressed in blue and white jockey's silks with a riding whip in his hand.

"Bloody 'ell, lad," he scolded. "What kind a hour d'ya call this? I'm 'avin' me portrait painted."

"I'm sorry ta inconvenience ya, Mr. Taylor, but I think I'm in strife."

Behind him Dolly appeared with a paintbrush in her hand. She seemed pleased to see me.

"Charlie," she shrieked. "Come inside at once!"

Pushing past Squizzy, she gave his backside a crack with the paintbrush, then took my arm and led me inside.

"Hang about, Doll," he protested. "What about the paintin'?"

Inside, the living room was set up like a racetrack, with a finishing post and all. Dolly gasped as I sat down next to her on the divan.

"Flamin' 'eck, Charlie. There's blood on yer shirt. . . . Look 'ere, Squiz, there's blood on Charlie's shirt."

Squizzy appeared with a glass of beer in his hand.

"What've ya been up ta, lad?"

His casual demeanor suggested he was no stranger to the claret.

"I clobbered a bloke with me cricket bat," I explained.

"What, were 'e droppin' 'em in short, were 'e? Yer've every right if 'e were bowlin' bouncers at yer."

"It were a man," I continued. "He was layin' inta me ma."

Beside me, Dolly reached for my hand.

"I've left 'im lyin' on the kitchen floor. There's blood comin' from 'is 'ead."

Squizzy rubbed his chin, deep in thought.

"Christ, Charlie, is there no end ta yer talents? Yer a fightin' man as well."

"Squizzy!"

"Awright, Doll, settle down."

Scolded, Squizzy sat in a chair opposite me and rested his beer on a nearby table.

"Let's 'ear it, then, Charlie."

With Dolly at my side, I told Squizzy all about the evening's events. I told him about Mr. Peacock and how he was once one of my father's closest friends, and I told him what he'd done to Ma.

Squizzy sat there listening, silently sipping his beer, until I was finished.

"So this Redmond fella—a neighbor, ya say—ya left 'im with yer ma?"

I nodded.

"And the bloke ya clobbered . . . ya saw 'im move 'is arm?"

"Yes."

Squizzy took a deep breath, then lifted himself out of the chair.

"I'll send someone over ta sit out the front, low-key, just in case this Peacock tosser wants ta go another round or two. In the meantime, Charlie, I want ya ta tell me everythin' ya know about 'im."

When I woke the next morning, I found myself trackside on Squizzy's divan. It felt late.

I lay there awhile, listening to the rain crashing onto the tin roof, until someone stirred behind me.

"I see that sleepin's another one a yer talents," chirped Squizzy.

"I'm sorry ta be such a bother, Mr. Taylor. I dunno how ta thank ya fer what ya done fer me."

"It's not me ya should be thankin', Charlie. It's Dolly. She's taken a real shine ta ya."

I looked around the room, expecting her to be there.

"She's nicked out fer a bit," he explained.

"Oh. . . . Would ya mind me askin' 'ow it went last night, then?"

"Me man picked up yer Mr. Peacock on 'is way ta see the coppers. He was all about pressin' charges."

"Charges?"

"Don't worry, I paid 'im a visit this mornin' at the timber yard. Had a nice little chat, we did. Put the fear a God up 'im. I think ya'll find that yer Mr. Peacock's sufferin' from amnesia. Can't remember a bloody thing."

"Ya mean I'm in the clear?" I asked.

"That ya are, Charlie. And 'e's 'ad a change a mind 'bout the wood as well. He'll be doin' 'is own rakin' from now on. Sat'd'y mornin's ya can 'elp yerself."

Right then, Squizzy reminded me of my father. Not in looks so much. It was more in the way he was able to make things right. I went to hug him, but he stopped me.

"Like I said, Charlie, it's Dolly ya should be thankin'. I suggest ya go 'ome and see yer ma."

When I arrived home, the kitchen floor had been wiped clean. Ma was standing at the sink with her back to me, feeding Jack something Mrs. Redmond had brought in.

I stood in the doorway, just as I had the night before. It felt strange being back there. It was so peaceful now.

I called out to Ma, but she didn't respond. Slowly I made my way to the sink, but she turned her face away as if to hide.

"Ma," I said softly.

Reluctantly she swung my way, and it was then that I saw her battered face. I was shocked. I took a step back and stood there looking, searching for my ma in the savaged face in front of me.

I could not believe that the woman standing before me was the same one who'd brought me into this world—the one who'd cared for me all these years. It wasn't possible.

But then, through swollen lips, I heard her whisper my name.

"Charlie."

Stepping forward, she drew me in with her free arm, and I went to her.

"I'm sorry, Charlie," she whispered again.

"It's awright, Ma. . . . Everythin's awright."

She was shaking, so I nestled into her and we stayed like that, the three of us, locked together for what seemed like forever.

CHAPTER TEN

It took a good week before Ma could see properly from her swollen eye. Even then she refused to leave the house. Shopping then became another chore I added to my list. So now, besides the long pants of adulthood, I was expected to wear a dress as well.

Ma made a joke about her face—something about not wanting to scare the neighbors' kids. But I knew there was more to it than that. She was a single woman now, and once the rumors had threaded their way through the streets of Richmond, they would have ended up so twisted they'd be saying that it was Ma who brought it on herself.

So instead she lay low and waited for the scars to heal. At first, the bruising seemed to be the worst of it. The skin around her bloodshot eye started off black and blue, like you'd expect. Then, as the days passed, all sorts of colors appeared. Up close you could see every color of the rainbow. There were greens, reds, purples, and yellows.

In the mornings, Ma stood in front of her bedroom mirror and dabbed white powder over her bruises. Every morning was the same. When she ventured out to the kitchen, it was my job to provide her with a daily update on her appearance.

"Well?" she'd ask.

"Good as new, Ma," I'd reply. "Ya'll be out dancin' soon."

In all honesty, I was surprised to see how well the powder softened her face, but it was not the bruises that concerned me most. The bruises, after all, would heal. It was something else— something that no amount of white powder could fix.

Ma had lost her smile.

We never talked about that night, Ma and I, not once. Whenever I tried to discuss it, she'd scurry off to another room as if she'd suddenly remembered an urgent chore that needed her attention. One time, I found her in the living room, dusting the doorknob with a rag. In her other hand was a metal ladle.

"What are ya doin', Ma?" I asked.

"I'm dustin', Charlie," she replied. "What does it look like I'm doin'?"

"Dustin'? What are ya doin' with a ladle, then?"

"Oh, that . . ."

Slowly Ma raised the ladle above her head and let her eyes wander across the floor.

"It's these blasted cockroaches," she said. "I just seen one, scootin' across the floor. As big as a tomcat, 'e was."

I took hold of her arm and held it tight.

"Why don't ya sit fer a while, Ma?" I said. "The 'ouse is spotless."

"Leave me be, Charlie. The place is a pigsty. What if someone comes visitin'?"

"Visitin'? That's a laugh. Why would anyone want ta come visitin'? Yer won't see anyone no more, and yer forever cleanin'. People want ta help, Ma. Why don't ya let 'em?"

She never looked at me anymore when she spoke. Instead, she chatted to the walls.

"Ma?" I pleaded.

I tugged at her arm and forced her to look at me. When she turned her head, I noticed the sickly white color in her face. Immediately I thought it was the Spanish flu that had ahold of her, but then I realized what it was. She'd begun covering not only the bruises but her entire face with powder.

"What are ya doin' ta yerself, Ma?" I pleaded. "It's been weeks now. There's powder all over yer face. There's no need fer it no more, the bruisin's cleared."

Slowly her vacant eyes left me and returned to the door-knob.

"Leave me be, Charlie. Just leave me be."

That's the way it was. In the mornings she covered her face with powder and she swept and cleaned, room after room. Then, when she'd run out of rooms, she'd start all over again.

Apart from my work with Squizzy, I dared not venture too far from the house, especially at night. Whenever I needed company, I found myself visiting the Redmonds next door. At least they were willing to talk.

"Yer the man a the 'ouse now, Charlie," Mrs. Redmond said one night. "I know it's a lot ta ask a someone so young, but yer ma'll be needin' ya ta be strong, what with 'er . . . condition an' all."

Her condition.

Although I was glad of the company, I hated the way Mrs. Redmond called it that. But it was more than just the word itself I objected to. It was the way she said it—the way she paused beforehand and looked around the room, as if there was something sinister about Ma's behavior.

When Mrs. Redmond talked like that, I found myself almost wishing the bruises back. At least then I could see what was wrong. But this condition, as she called it—I knew it was something in Ma's head. And it scared me.

Another thing that troubled me was the way Mrs. Redmond always referred to me as "the man of the house." True, I had been wearing my father's boots for some months now. Wearing them was easy. All I had to do was slide them on and lace them up. Any mug who knew the art of tying laces could do that. But filling them, now that was a different story altogether.

One night while the Redmonds were fixing a cup of tea in their kitchen, Mr. Redmond returned to the living room and caught me standing in front of the mirror with my shirtsleeves rolled up, checking myself for muscles.

"So?" he asked. "What's the verdict?"

"I'm only sixteen, Mr. Redmond," I answered. "I don't think I'm ready ta be the man a the 'ouse just yet."

"Ya 'aven't done a bad job of it so far, Charlie. Personally, I'd think twice before messin' with ya, after what I seen the other night."

"That were a lucky shot, I reckon. Anyway, I'd look a bit of a dill walkin' around the place with a cricket bat tucked under me arm."

"Listen, 'ave ya ever thought 'bout boxin', Charlie?"

"Boxin'?"

"Yeah. I did a bit meself when I were yer age. I could train ya if ya want."

"Could ya?"

"Don't see why not. Ya got the runnin' in yer legs already. We could start tomorra night, if ya like."

. . .

Next day as I ran an errand down Little Lonsdale Street, I heard a voice inside my head.

Ladies and gentlemen, it said. *May I present the middleweight champion of the world . . . Mr. Charlie Feehan.*

I pulled up in front of a tailor's shop, and just for fun I gave the mannequin outside a quick one-two combination—left, right. *Bang, bang.*

Stunned, the mannequin failed to respond. Already I could sense he was in trouble, so I moved quickly to the left, dropped my shoulder, and hammered my right fist up into his rib cage. It was a Charlie Feehan special, poor bugger.

Just as I was about to finish him off, something made contact with my left ear. I turned and saw an angry shopkeeper standing in front of me with her hands on her hips.

"Ouch," I cried. "That bloody well 'urt, missus."

"Good. And I'll give ya another one if ya don't leave off."

For a moment I thought about telling her that future middleweight champions deserved more respect, but something in her face warned me against it. Instead I continued up Little Lonsdale with a ringing noise in my ear.

That night I wolfed down my mutton flaps and potato, then scurried next door for my first training session with Mr. Redmond.

He'd been busy. The first thing I noticed was the punching bag hanging from the back verandah. Seeing it, I raced over and started laying into it with my fists.

After a few seconds, Mr. Redmond grabbed hold of my arm. "Easy does it, champ," he said. "Yer not ready fer the bag."

"Where'd ya get it?" I asked.

"It's Bert O'Meara's kit bag from the war. He's got no use fer it no more. He's full a mustard gas, poor bugger. I've filled it full a sand."

I nodded respectfully, remembering the time Bert had called in to our house to share a beer with my father just before he left for the battlefields of France. He was a giant of a man, thickset like a draft horse. My father had often joked that Bert O'Meara was the only man at Victoria Dock who could unload an entire ship's cargo with his bare hands before the lunch bell sounded. But now that same man was a mere skeleton, and like my father, he too would suffer the indignity of dying in bed, between piss-stained sheets.

I looked at Bert's bag, still swinging from the verandah.

"What d'ya mean, I'm not ready fer the bag? I'm 'ere fer the boxin', Mr. Redmond, remember?"

"First thing ya gotta learn, Charlie, there's more ta boxin' than punchin'."

"There is?" I asked. "Like what?"

"Like the two F's, finkin' and footwork. It's all up 'ere," he said, pointing to his head. "Ya'll not be punchin' the bag till yer ready."

With that, he handed me a training list.

I had no problem with the first entry, running. Even the next two, push-ups and sit-ups, seemed sensible enough. It was the fourth entry I had trouble with.

"Skippin'?" I asked in disbelief. "Crikey, Mr. Redmond, next ya'll be tellin' me there's knittin' involved."

Mr. Redmond smiled, then made his way to a wooden chest on the verandah.

"There's no knittin', is there, Mr. Redmond?"

From the wooden chest Mr. Redmond pulled out a skipping rope and tossed it to me.

"No, Charlie, there's no knittin'. But there could be a spot a sewin' needed if I 'ear any more whingein' outta ya. Here, see what ya can do with this."

I untangled the rope and found two large knots at either end. All over Richmond, the streets and schoolyards were full of girls skipping, but in all my years I'd never had the need to pay much attention to the technicalities of jumping rope. As I moved to the center of the yard, Mrs. Redmond appeared on the back verandah.

"What fun," she said. "I 'aven't done any skippin' since I were a girl. How 'bout I count ya in, Charlie?"

With the rope resting behind my heels, I was ready to begin. I looked up at Mrs. Redmond, who'd taken a seat on the wooden chest.

"Ya ready?" she asked.

I nodded.

"A one, and a two, and a one, two, three."

I was away.

Surprisingly, I managed to jump the first four in a row, and perhaps it would have been more had Mrs. Redmond not started singing. "Pat a cake, pat a cake, baker's man, bake me a cake as fast as you can."

On the fourth jump, when the rope hit the back of my boots, I stopped and gathered it in one hand. It was time to make a stand.

"Why've ya stopped, Charlie?" asked Mr. Redmond.

I held my ground in the middle of the yard and waved Mr. Redmond over.

"Listen, I'm not whinin' or nothin'," I whispered. "But it's Mrs. Redmond. She's puttin' me off. Do we 'ave ta 'ave nursery rhymes while I'm skippin'?"

With his hand on his chin, Mr. Redmond glanced over his shoulder toward the verandah.

"I'm afraid so, Charlie. Unless ya want ta start yer sparrin' practice early. Mrs. Redmond's a bit sensitive about her singin'. I suggest ya try and think about somethin' else."

As I stepped back into position, I tried to follow Mr. Redmond's advice, but all I could think about was Les Darcy, Australia's champion middleweight boxer. I bet he never had nursery rhymes.

On my next attempt I jumped five, then six, then eight. I was getting better by the minute, and although I hated to admit it, I found Mrs. Redmond's nursery rhymes actually helping me with my rhythm. That night I left the Redmonds' with a record fifteen jumps in a row. Soon I'd be ready for the bag.

CHAPTER ELEVEN

Nostrils was impressed. About the boxing, I mean. When I met him on Saturday morning, I told him all about the training.

"So yer 'ittin' the bag?" he asked.

"Course I'm 'ittin' the bag," I lied. "It's boxin'. What did ya think I'd be doin', dancin'?"

"Maybe I could join ya. It'd 'elp me with me footy. I'm playin' this arvo. They've picked me on the forward flank."

Suddenly a familiar song sounded in my head: *Pat a cake, pat a cake, baker's man. . . .*

"Er . . . I'll ask Mr. Redmond fer ya, Nostrils, but I'm pretty sure he's not after takin' on any others. Besides, it ain't as simple as kickin' a footy 'round an oval. Ya should see some a the things he's got me doin'. There's no muckin' 'bout, ya know. What I'm doin' is a science."

Soon the two of us arrived at Stone's Timber Yard. It was the first time since the beating that I'd had the courage to resume the wood run, and I don't mind admitting that the thought of seeing Mr. Peacock again had me feeling as edgy as a stray chook on Christmas Day. Still, at least I had Nostrils with me.

I stopped at the gate and took a couple of deep breaths.

"Ya awright, Charlie?" asked Nostrils. "Ya don't look so good."

"Yeah, I'm awright," I answered. "I'm just 'opin' that Squizzy's sorted things."

Grabbing hold of my trolley's handle, I held my head high and strode through the front gate. As we passed the foreman's hut on our left, the door slammed shut. I couldn't look.

"That Peacock fella," said Nostrils. "What's 'e done ta 'imself? He's got a bandage 'round 'is 'ead."

Normally I had no trouble coming clean where Nostrils was concerned. He was my best friend now, after all. But here my hands were tied.

"Dunno," I lied. "Maybe someone's clocked 'im one. About time, I reckon. Come on, Nostrils, 'ow 'bout we load up and get outta 'ere."

We loaded up all right—two trolleys full. While Mr. Peacock sat stewing in his grotty little hut, Nostrils and I helped ourselves to the wood stack. You cannot imagine the pleasure it gave me, hurling log after log into the trolleys. They were big logs, too, none of the splinters like before. And when our trolleys could not take any more, I picked up a twig and drew a message in the dirt: UP YOURS, PEACOCK.

That afternoon when I arrived at the Heaths', I found Nostrils nuggeting his footy boots. Compared to his father, Nostrils seemed fairly relaxed.

"Thank God yer 'ere, Charlie," said Mr. Heath as I entered the living room. "Pull up a seat. I'm just runnin' through some last-minute instructions with Norman 'ere. But fer the life a me, I'm sure there's somethin' I've fergotten. D'ya 'ave any words a wisdom of yer own?"

Pat a cake, pat a cake, baker's man. . . .

There was that blasted song again.

"Um . . . 'ave ya told 'im about the two F's at all?" I asked.

Mr. Heath slapped his knee.

"Of course!" he said. "The two F's. I knew there were somethin'."

As I looked around the room for sponge cake, I felt a hand on my forearm. Beside me, Mr. Heath looked confused.

"Er, I'm familiar with it meself, a course, Charlie, but I might get ya ta explain it ta Norman 'ere. What exactly are the two F's?"

"The two F's," I said casually. "Finkin' and footwork."

During my brief explanation, I couldn't help feeling that Nostrils and his father were having difficulty fully grasping the ins and outs of the two F's. I shouldn't have been surprised, I suppose. After all, the stuff I was telling them was highly technical in its nature—stuff that was difficult to digest for those without a bit of boxing know-how like myself.

Still, a little more enthusiasm would have been nice.

When I was done, Mr. Heath looked none the wiser.

"Ya'd better make that three F's, Charlie," he scoffed. "That were the biggest load a frogshit I ever 'eard. Ignore 'im, Norman. When ya get yer 'ands on the ball, kick the bloody thing long."

When the four of us arrived at the oval opposite the Punt Road ground, a large crowd was already gathered. For the people of Richmond, footy at any level was worth getting excited about, especially when one of the teams was wearing black and yellow.

There was an icy southerly howling across the oval, left

to right, and as usual it was Mr. Heath doing most of the talking.

"I've got another *F* ta add ta yer list, Charlie," he said, smirking. "It's bloody freezin'."

Ever since we'd left Nostrils' place, Mr. Heath was throwing *F*'s at me thick and fast. By now the two *F*'s had swelled to eight.

"Ya'd better steady on, Mr. Heath," I countered. "I'll be runnin' outta fingers before long."

Soon enough it was time for Nostrils to join the rest of his teammates in the change rooms.

"Awright, then, I'd best be off. I'll see yis after the game." He smiled.

Mrs. Heath, who'd been unusually quiet, gave her son a quick hug.

"Ya'll be right, love," she whispered.

Next in line was Mr. Heath. He grabbed hold of Norman's hand and shook it firmly.

"There's a breeze blowin', Norman," he said. "Make sure yer thinkin' 'bout the breeze when yer linin' up the sticks."

I was next. I slid my hand into Nostrils' and tried to think of something clever to say. Nothing came. All I could remember was that day in the park.

"Yer Vic Thorp, remember. Yer a freak."

With his bag tucked under his arm, Nostrils made his way to the rooms, and for the first time I noticed something about him. There was a gracefulness in his stride. Even when some rowdy punter blocked his path, Nostrils simply shifted his weight and danced around him.

Class.

That was what they called it. And Nostrils had it in spades.
Beside me Mr. Heath leaned my way and spoke.

"Freak, ya said. If I'm not mistaken, that'd make it nine."

The team from Fitzroy came out first, and as they ran onto the
oval I remembered why it was I'd never taken to footy. Except
for a couple of smaller roving types, most of them were giants—
more like grown men than boys. I tell you, it wouldn't have surprised me none if some of them had a wife and kids waiting for
them at home.

Not far to my right, a group of supporters started making
some noise, and as I looked their way a flash of red in the middle of the crowd caught my eye. I rested my hand on Mr.
Heath's shoulder and lifted myself onto my toes for a better
look.

"'Em's the opposition supporters, Charlie," he said. "Why
don't ya concentrate on somethin' else?"

There it was again. A mop of dazzling red hair. I lifted
myself even higher and discovered that the owner of those
flaming locks was a girl of similar age to myself.

"Carn the Roys!" she screamed.

If Mr. Heath hadn't brushed my hand from his shoulder, I
might well have missed Nostrils running out.

"Get yer hands off me, Charlie," he snapped. "The lads are
on their way out."

Richmond Hill came out single file, and like the Fitzroy
team, they too were big. I spotted Nostrils in the middle of the
line wearing number twelve on his back. I wasn't normally the
vocal type, but seeing Nostrils in the yellow and black got me
excited.

"Eat 'em alive, Tigers!" I roared.

After a series of warm-ups, the players moved into position, and by sheer good fortune I noticed Nostrils striding to the flank in front of us.

He looked sharp.

"Attaboy, Nostrils," I bellowed.

This time it was Mrs. Heath who found my ear.

"If ya don't mind, Charlie," she said, "I'd prefer it if ya called 'im Norman. It's more professional."

As I saw it, I had a few spare minutes up my sleeve before the ball was bounced, so I went about locating the girl with the fiery hair. I'd just spotted her when Mr. Heath started chewing my other ear.

"He don't look that tough," he said.

Without turning, I grunted a reply. "Huh?"

Again his hand found my shoulder.

"Will ya bloody well stop pervin' at the opposition and concentrate on the game, Charlie?"

Reluctantly I dragged my eyes from the girl and faced him.

"Sorry, Mr. Heath. What was it ya were sayin'?"

"Norman's opponent." He pointed. "He don't look so tough ta me. What d'ya think?"

I don't know why I did it—after all, I was a good forty feet from the flank—but when I saw Nostrils' opponent I ducked for cover behind Mrs. Heath.

"Bloody 'ell, it's Jimmy Barlow."

"Ya know 'im?"

"I'm afraid I do, Mr. Heath. He's as tough as nails."

Suddenly a whistle sounded, and while those around me looked to the center square, I kept my eyes on the flank.

Seconds into the game, Barlow made his intentions clear. Just as the Tigers went into attack, he lifted his elbow high across his body, then brought it down hard into Nostrils' stomach.

He was going the knuckle.

With the wind taken out of him, Nostrils dropped onto one knee and began gasping for air.

"What the flamin' 'eck's he doin'?" said Mr. Heath. "He's picked a bloody fine time ta get religious. Couldn't he 'ave done his prayin' before the game?"

All through the first half, Barlow had Nostrils off his game. Whenever the black and yellow came forward, Nostrils would try to match his opponent with strength. And while his refusal to take a backward step was admirable, he seemed to be losing sight of what was most important—possession.

When the halftime whistle sounded, Fitzroy was up by sixteen points. Mr. Heath looked tense.

"I'll be back in a jiff," he said. "There's somethin' I gotta tell Norman."

Crashing through the crowd, Mr. Heath caught up with his son and slung an arm around his shoulder. It was a simple thing, something that my own father had done with me. Now, as I stood there watching them in the crowd, I felt a sharp pang of grief. Never again, I realized, would I experience my father's touch.

Soon enough, the players emerged for the second half, and once again Nostrils made his way over to Barlow on the flank. As soon as they came together, Barlow was into him, bumping chests and pulling on his jumper. But unlike during the first half, Nostrils simply pushed him aside and kept his eyes fixed on the action in the center square.

When the ball was bounced, Richmond's ruckman palmed off a perfect tap to the waiting rover, who kicked it forward. Quickly I looked to the flank and saw Nostrils drop his shoulder into Barlow, sending him sideways. With his opponent off balance, Nostrils charged after the ball and gathered it up with one hand. Speeding toward the goal, he took a bounce, then another.

"Attaboy, Norman," screamed Mr. Heath. "'Ave a shot, son."

Oozing class, Nostrils slowed up, then dropped the ball onto his right boot. At first it looked as though he'd aimed it too far left, but as it sailed into the air the breeze got hold of it and pushed it right, straight through the big sticks.

Goal!

Before I knew what was happening, I was dancing a jig with Mr. and Mrs. Heath, right there in the middle of the crowd.

"I dunno what ya told 'im, Mr. Heath," I said, "but it sure seems to 'ave worked."

"I 'ope ya don't mind, Charlie, but I borrowed one a yer F's."

"Ya did?"

"Yeah." He smiled. "I told 'im to start finkin' smart."

All through the second half, Nostrils took Barlow apart. Whenever the ball entered Richmond's forward line, Nostrils was there. He outplayed him, not with muscle, but with speed and skill. One on one, when it came to getting the footy, Barlow was no match. He simply couldn't keep up.

When the whistle sounded to signal the end of the game, Richmond Hill, thanks largely to Nostrils' devastating second half, had won by twenty-two points.

As the players left the field, I decided it was time to get a closer look at the girl with the red hair. While Mr. and Mrs. Heath took off to congratulate their son, I hung back and mingled with the opposition.

Next to me a girl in a gray coat cupped a hand around her mouth.

"Hey, Alice," she called. "Let's get goin'."

Slowly the red-haired girl turned and began walking my way. Soon she was next to me, close enough to touch, and for a second I thought about saying something. I even opened my mouth. But, as usual, nothing came.

Seeing her up close, however, I realized that her hair was only the half of it. She was beautiful. Her cheeks were soft and shiny pink, and her delicate nose was dotted with freckles so perfect it was as if someone had gathered them up between thumb and forefinger and sprinkled them gently across her face.

Alice.

She was past me now. Gone. And, even though I'd been unable to make an impression, I caught myself smiling.

For the moment, at least, I had everything I needed.

I had her name.

CHAPTER TWELVE

When I woke on Monday morning, there was a freckle-faced girl with wild hair on my wall. Smiling, I rolled onto my back and began filling my head with her.

I took myself back to Saturday's game and replayed that final moment with Alice, only this time as she walked toward me she smiled and touched my arm. I was all set to say something when a noise from the kitchen killed the moment.

Ma was up.

Halfway along the hall I stopped at the living room door and found her on her hands and knees, running the tip of a knife along a join in the floorboards.

"What are ya doin', Ma?" I asked.

"Ya'd never believe 'ow much dirt gets into these 'ere cracks," she said without looking up. "I'll 'ave a few trolley loads fer ya before I'm done."

I stood there in the doorway awhile and watched my ma groveling on her hands and knees, tut-tutting every time she dislodged a sizeable clump of dirt. When she was like this, with her mind on the cleaning, nothing I could say would make her stop. Part of me wanted to hurl myself onto the floor and snatch the knife away, but I knew that as soon as I was gone she'd have found herself a new one.

As the weeks passed, Ma's condition seemed to get worse. Unlike before, she hardly raised an eyebrow when I returned from the timber yard with my trolley full of logs, and when I handed her the doctored report card from Mrs. Nagle, she looked at it as if it were a shopping list. But it was Jack I worried about the most. If it hadn't been for Mrs. Redmond, I tell you, I don't know how we would have managed.

That morning I found him in the corner of the kitchen, asleep in his bassinet. I hadn't time to fix myself breakfast, so I walked over to say goodbye. As I bent down to kiss his cheek, I saw a cockroach at the corner of his mouth, feeding on a patch of crusty milk.

Without thinking, I reached in and snatched it up. In my haste to remove the roach, my fingernails tore some skin from his cheek. As I squashed the roach between my fingers, Jack opened his eyes and began to howl.

When I arrived at Squizzy's place that morning, Dolly met me at the door.

"He's in a foul mood this mornin', Charlie," she whispered, craning her head toward the office inside. "Ya'd better 'ave yer wits 'bout ya. Somethin's gone wrong."

She was right. Only two steps into the hallway, Squizzy blew his top.

"Who the bloody 'ell does 'e think 'e is?" he roared. "If it's a scrap 'e's wantin', I'll give it to 'im, awright. I'll fill the weasel full a holes."

The next voice I heard was Dasher's.

"Calm yerself down, Squiz. It's only rumors I'm passin' on.

Why don't ya pour yerself a whisky? It might help settle yer nerves."

"Good thinkin', Dash. . . . Dolly! Get off yer arse and fetch us two whiskies. Make 'em doubles. And while yer at it, ya can fix us a sandwich as well."

While Dolly delivered the whiskies, I crept toward the living room door and pressed my ear hard against it.

"I tell ya, Dash, if Snowy Cutmore's after mixin' it with me, he's in fer one 'ell of a stoush. I'll take on the whole a Fitzroy if I 'ave ta."

"Look, Squiz," said Dasher, "before ya do anythin' rash, 'ow about we send someone in ta see what they're up ta? Ya might be overreactin'."

"Me? Overreactin'? They're bad-mouthin' me, all over town. I won't 'ave it. I've a reputation ta consider."

"It's just what I 'eard, Squiz. They're sayin' ya shortchanged 'em with the takin's from the jewelry job in Kew."

"Too bloody right I did. It was me and Matt Daly what did the joint over. I only let Cutmore shift the stuff ta get 'im off me back. Sniffin' around like a shit'ouse rat, 'e was."

"I'm afraid there's more," said Dasher.

"Strike me pink, ya full a good news, ya are. C'mon, then, let's 'ear it."

"Cutmore's been seen drinkin' with Micky Morgan."

"And?"

"Micky Morgan, Squiz. Ya wanna think careful before ya go startin' somethin'. Morgan's as mad as a cut snake."

"I'll not be bendin' over fer no one, Dash. If the two of 'em wanna play handies, let 'em. That Fitzroy push are a pack a sheilas. Always 'ave been."

A pause in the conversation told me that Dolly had arrived with the sandwiches, so I stepped away from the door and thought about what I'd just heard.

Snowy Cutmore was well known as a man with a violent streak. Rumor had it that one night, in the company of a young lass and with a skinful of liquor under his belt, he took to her rump with a branding iron after she steadfastly refused his advances. Blue-eyed and blond-haired, he was one of the king-pins of the Fitzroy push—an unpredictable man with a liking for a scrap. Put simply, messing with Snowy Cutmore was bad for your health.

Then there was Morgan, known around the traps as "Tramlines" on account of the two scars down his left cheek. Morgan was Fitzroy's equivalent of Henry Stokes. He ran his two-up schools with such a tight fist that it wasn't uncommon for punters in Fitzroy to make their way to Richmond, to Goodwood Street in particular, where the atmosphere was more relaxed.

Though many had tried, no one yet had gone up against Cutmore and won. And now with Tramlines standing beside him, victory seemed near impossible. Don't get me wrong—despite his size, Squizzy Taylor was no pushover himself. But as I stood there in his living room, something told me that this time Squizzy Taylor was fighting outside his weight.

As soon as I'd changed into my new black boots, Squizzy summoned me, none too politely.

"Where's that flamin' runner?" he bellowed from his office. "Charlie! Get yerself in 'ere."

Stepping into the office, I found Squizzy pacing the room with a whisky glass in his hand. From the look of him, he hadn't slept.

"Sorry, Mr. Taylor," I said. "I thought ya was in a meetin'."

"Flamin' 'ell, lad, I'm not payin' ya ta be thinkin'."

Standing at the desk, he ran his fingers through his hair and with his free hand shuffled through some papers.

"And I'm not payin' ya ta be sittin' 'round on yer arse, either. Yer as bad as Dolly. The two a ya are wearin' 'oles in the furniture. 'Struth, the guests'll be fallin' through the chairs before long."

He was frantic now, pushing papers across the desk.

"Where the flamin' 'ell did I put that list?" he roared. "It was sittin' right 'ere when I turned me back. Dasher, if yer playin' funny buggers with me, I'll 'ave yer."

Finally he spotted what he was looking for on the left-hand corner of his desk.

"Awright, Charlie, now listen up. I've written down on this paper 'ere a list a people what owe me money. Next ta the address is the amount owin'. Normally I'd be goin' ta collect it meself, but I've other things on me mind right now, and I want the boys ready if any trouble starts."

I nodded.

"It's quite straightforward. Yer ta visit each of these addresses and tell 'em that yer've come ta collect Mr. Taylor's money. Got it?"

I nodded again.

"If any of 'em start messin' ya 'round, yer ta tell 'em from me that if I 'ave ta come down in person, I won't be callin' in fer tea and biscuits."

With that, Squizzy handed me the list. There were six names in total, each of them accompanied by an address. Quickly I ran through them in my head, then stopped at the last entry.

"Somethin' wrong?" asked Squizzy.

"There seems ta be some mistake with the last entry, Mr. Taylor," I replied nervously. "It says 'ere it's in Fitzroy."

"There's no mistake, Charlie."

"So yer wantin' me ta go inta Fitzroy?"

Beside me Dasher drained the contents of his whisky glass, then sat up in his chair.

"Don't worry, Charlie," he told me with a grimace. "No one knows ya in Fitzroy. It's better that you be goin' than one a us."

Collecting Squizzy Taylor's outstanding debts was a dangerous occupation in itself, especially for a lad of sixteen years. But in a suburb like Fitzroy, where a large number of his enemies resided, Squizzy Taylor was now about as popular as a dose of the Spanish flu.

With the instructions clear in my head, I headed down the hall and out the front door. Already I'd decided to leave the Fitzroy address until last, so I tucked the list into a pocket and began running at an easy pace toward the city.

Although I was mindful of the miles I had to cover, today I felt strong. By the time I'd reached Punt Road, my legs had settled into a comfortable rhythm, leaving me free to think about the day ahead.

The collecting of debts was usually a two-man job, and in Squizzy's push those two men were Billy Tobin and Knuckles Lonergan. Billy, although slight of build, was a man with a razor-sharp tongue. He was the front man, the spruiker, and seldom failed to persuade a shopkeeper to hand over whatever amount was owing. But if for some reason the shopkeeper refused, Knuckles, all six foot four of him, would step in with the muscle.

Today, however, I was on my own. I had none of Billy's persuasive talents. In fact, I couldn't guarantee that my own tongue would be working at all, what with its habit of taking unauthorized naps.

And muscle?

There was the odd bump here and there, but you'd be stretching the truth to be calling them muscles. So, unless a shopkeeper called on me for a dodgy display of skipping, I had no idea how to tackle the job.

Finally, as I headed up Spring Street, I settled on a plan: polite but firm. It wasn't much, but it was all I had.

At the Eastern Market in Bourke Street, I slowed to a walk and unfolded the list in my pocket. The first entry said, *Albert Fox—greengrocer, 111 Bourke Street, £3.*

I stepped nervously through the main entrance, past the tattooist and the shooting gallery, and made my way to the lower quadrangle, where I knew the grocer to be. Nearing the stall, I spotted a man outside arranging some apples into neat rows. Albert Fox was much younger than I'd imagined. I'd been hoping for someone older first up, someone who'd give up the money as soon as I asked. And this Albert Fox, he was big.

I stood with my eyes closed for a few moments and took a couple of deep breaths.

"Polite but firm," I said softly. "Polite but firm."

Slowly I walked over until I was behind him.

"Mr. Albert Fox?" I asked.

He answered without turning, keeping his eyes on the apples. "Who wants ta know?"

"I've come ta collect Mr. Taylor's money," I said.

Suddenly I had his attention, and he began eyeing me suspiciously.

"Is that so?"

"It is, sir. And I'd be appreciatin' it if ya could attend ta the matter directly. I've a busy day ahead."

Hooking his thumbs through his apron straps, Mr. Fox broke into a smile, then raised his voice.

"And what makes ya think I'd be willin' ta fork over me 'ard-earned ta a pipsqueak like you?"

"I can think of one good reason, Mr. Fox. If Mr. Taylor has ta come down 'ere with Knuckles in tow, they won't be sittin' down fer tea and biscuits. I've just come from Mr. Taylor's place and I can tell ya, he's itchin' ta do 'is block."

In front of me Mr. Fox put away his smile and unhooked his thumbs.

Polite but firm—it was working.

"Awright, awright," he whined. "Keep yer flamin' shirt on. I'll go and fetch it."

As he retreated into the shop, a wave of bravado rose in my chest. I reached down and grabbed an apple, then tossed it into the air. When it landed in my right hand, I lifted it up to my mouth and took a healthy bite.

Before long Mr. Fox reappeared and joined me at the front of the shop.

"It's a pleasure doin' business with ya," I said, taking the envelope from his outstretched hand. "And by the way, them apples—they're a bit on the green side."

CHAPTER THIRTEEN

After my successful encounter with Albert Fox, I went about collecting Squizzy's money as if Knuckles himself was standing beside me. I never once stopped to think about what I was doing—about the people on the list. All that mattered was the money.

At each of the city addresses it was the same. When they first saw me, they resisted, but once I'd mentioned the tea and biscuits, all I had to do was hold out my hand.

Now for Fitzroy.

With the money tucked safely in my pocket, I made it to the top end of town and headed toward Brunswick Street. Although buoyed by my early success, I was still clearheaded enough to know that things in Fitzroy would be different.

My last stop, according to the list, was a cake shop in Johnston Street. The name was Kenneth Cornwall.

From Brunswick Street I turned right into Johnston and kept walking. On the opposite side of the street, some twenty yards away, I spotted the shop. Next door, a group of three men were slouching in front of a billiard hall, smoking.

In many ways, Fitzroy was a lot like Richmond. Its main streets were abuzz with the sound of clunking trams and the clip-clop of horses' hooves. As a newcomer, seeing its shops and hotels for the first time, you'd be fooled into thinking that here was a vibrant and bustling suburb. But if you were to scratch beneath the surface and stroll behind the rosy facade, you'd soon discover an underbelly of a different sort. For the people who resided in the back streets and narrows of Fitzroy, living was the easy part. It was surviving that was the trick.

In the fifteen minutes I'd been staking out the cake shop, the only thing to have changed was my mood. The early cockiness I'd felt as I ran around the city had all but disappeared, and my chest, once full of bravado, was now deflated to its original size.

I wasn't close enough to see inside the shop, so I settled my nerves by telling myself that bakers, on the whole, weren't known for having a vicious streak. Bakers baked. They wore aprons and caps and had smudges of flour on the tips of their noses.

I was stalling.

Two more cars, I told myself. After two more cars motored by, I'd launch myself off the footpath and march straight into the shop.

Easy.

Not surprisingly, two cars became three. Three became four, then six, then eight.

Finally, I mustered enough courage to make a move. I stepped into the gutter and ambled across Johnston Street toward the shop.

Polite but firm.

I smiled at the men in front of the billiard hall and pushed quietly through the cake shop door. In the glass cabinet in front of me, a girl wearing a hat was bent low, adding some sticky sweets to the cake display. She hadn't seen me, so I tapped on the glass near her head.

"Afternoon," I said.

Startled, she rose and hit her head on the shelf above her. *Crunch.*

With her hand clutching her head, she emerged from the cabinet and straightened up.

The first thing I saw was the freckles.

"What are ya thinkin', sneakin' up on a girl like that?" she said crossly.

I was stunned. I wasn't ready to be meeting Alice so soon. I had nothing prepared.

"Er . . ."

"Well?"

I could think of nothing interesting to say, so I blurted out the first thing that came to mind.

"I've got the taste fer one a them cakes there," I said, pointing to my right. "I'll take that big fella at the back, if ya don't mind."

Alice seemed unimpressed. She rolled her eyes, then tucked a loose ringlet of red hair back underneath her hat.

Inside I was dying.

"That'll be threepence," she said, handing it to me.

I took it from her, then dropped a couple of coins into her hand. I had to redeem myself. I took a step back and bit into the creamy bun.

"They're not 'alf bad," I said. "What d'ya call 'em?"

"Cream buns, genius."

Standing there in the shop, I realized that if I was to have any chance with Alice, the next thing to leave my mouth would have to be something special. Time had come to start finkin' smart. I swallowed the last of the bun and began to think about the women in my life. There were Ma, Mrs. Redmond, and Dolly. It was by no means a lengthy list, but at the same time it occurred to me that all three women had something in common. They were all attracted to men who could make them laugh. While there wasn't a great deal to smile about when you lived in the slums, laughing was one of the few things that came for free.

At this stage in our relationship I was under no illusion as to where I stood with Alice. She was giving me the cold shoulder something shocking. Even if I'd started doing cartwheels across the shop floor, I doubt whether she would have paid me the slightest attention. I had to make a move, and I had to do it now.

Slowly I stepped forward and positioned myself at the end of the counter. My plan, if you could call it that, was to start up a conversation; then, when the moment presented itself, I would catch her off guard with a witty remark.

Polite but firm was out. Funny was in.

Behind the counter Alice was busy stacking loaves, so I coughed gently into my hand to remind her I was still there. I was all ready to start something when out of the corner of my eye I spotted a familiar figure outside the shop window. It was Barlow. Quickly my survival instincts cut in, and I dropped to the floor and crawled behind the counter. Right then, I knew I'd blown it with Alice. I sat at her feet, cowering like a frightened puppy.

She was about to protest when I raised a finger up to my lips.

"Shhhhhhhhh!"

Sure enough, the shop door opened and in stepped trouble.

"How ya goin', Alice?" called Barlow. "Yer lookin' well today."

Beside me Alice's body stiffened.

"What d'ya want?" she asked.

"'Struth, that's a nice how-d'ya-do. I'm 'ere ta take two a them pies off yer 'ands."

For a second I thought about showing myself and making a stand. I'd often wondered, seeing the wounded soldiers return home from the fighting abroad, how I would have fared had I been old enough to sling a rifle over my shoulder. Now I knew.

While Alice fetched the pies, I lay low and buried my head. On the other side of the counter, Barlow began sniffing.

"I s'pose ya'll be along ta see me this Sat'd'y, then?" he said. "We're playin' at 'ome."

"I'll be goin' awright," said Alice, "but it's not you I'll be lookin' at. Ya got murdered last week. Cost us the game, I reckon."

With my back against the counter, I thought of Nostrils and smiled.

"He were lucky, that bloke. I'll fix 'im up next time we play 'em, don't worry about that."

With the transaction complete, Barlow took the pies and stepped toward the door.

"By the way," he said, "if ya change yer mind 'bout goin' ta the flicks, ya know where ta find me."

After the door closed, Alice dropped the coins into the register.

"Thanks fer that," I said. "I take it yer not all that keen on Jimmy Barlow."

"He's a tosser. He thinks he can push people 'round just because he's done a bit a boxin'."

"Ya don't like boxin'?"

"I hate it."

My father had taught me many things when he was alive. He'd told me that a true test of character was not the number of times a man got knocked to the ground. After all, life packed a punch like nothing else. A true test of a man's character was in his ability to pick himself up.

Character-wise, I'd failed to rack up a single point in the last half hour. I sat against the counter and reeled in my legs. Instead of passing by me, Alice stopped and placed her hands on her hips.

"Listen, it's been real fun havin' ya here, but yer really gettin' on me nerves now. If yer not goin' ta buy anythin', get outta me way, will ya? I've work ta do."

Sitting there with my knees hard up against my chest, I suddenly remembered why it was I'd come into the shop in the first place.

"Cripes!"

Even though it was a little late for heroics, I picked myself up off the floor and walked back around the counter.

"Do ya by any chance 'ave a Kenneth Cornwall workin' here?" I asked.

Alice looked surprised.

"Kenneth Cornwall?" she asked. "What's it to ya?"

"I'd like a word in his ear, if I could."

Finally I had her attention. It was the moment I'd been waiting for all afternoon. I'd dreamt of this moment, but now, as she fixed me with her beautiful brown eyes, I tell you, I felt mighty uncomfortable.

Slowly she turned, then waltzed toward the rear door, pushed it open, and yelled, "Dad, there's someone out 'ere wants a word with ya."

Suddenly the cream bun in my gut began making a move.

"Dad?" I asked.

"That's right. I'm Alice Cornwall."

For a few seconds I stood there, stunned. I considered going to ground behind the counter again, only this time Alice was on to me. As I ducked my head, she scurried back and stood with her arms folded, blocking my path.

"Ah, no ya don't."

Clearly, bolting was my only option. I was all set to leave when Kenneth Cornwall poked his head through the rear door.

"Who is it, Alice?"

"Er . . ."

Alice looked to me for a name.

"Charlie Feehan," I whispered.

"He says 'is name is Charlie Feehan."

"What's 'e want?"

I had no reason to doubt that the head in the doorway belonged to Alice's father, but the way it bobbed when it spoke, the whole thing reminded me of a puppet show. It was as if the head itself was attached to a stick.

"I'd like a word with ya, Mr. Cornwall," I said. "In private, if ya don't mind?"

For a second the bobbing stopped.

"Awright, then," he answered. "Ya can come out back."

I smiled at Alice and walked slowly to the rear of the shop. A few yards from the doorway I felt the warmth radiating from the ovens in the back room. The sweet smell of baking bread hung so thick in the air I could almost taste it.

Farther in, Kenneth Cornwall, complete with arms and legs, stood leaning on a bench to my left, a cigarette tucked behind his ear. Straightaway my eyes were drawn to his face. I couldn't explain it at first, but as I stepped closer I began to understand the reason for my fascination. Alice was her father's daughter. Dead spit.

Up close I could see her in his face—the brown eyes, the red hair, and the freckles. But Kenneth Cornwall looked tired. He had none of Alice's fire about him. In his eyes I saw none of her spark, not even a flicker.

"What d'ya want?" he asked.

"I'm here fer Mr. Taylor's money."

"I ain't got it," he replied.

Before I could give him the tea-and-bickies spiel, Kenneth Cornwall lifted himself off the bench and hobbled toward the oven with a limp so severe he reminded me of a penguin. As he opened the oven door, I shifted my eyes to his feet and noticed the sole of his left boot was a good two inches thicker than the one on his right.

"What are ya gawkin' at?" he barked.

"Nothin', sir. I were just—"

"I know what ya were doin'. Ya were gawkin'. Ain't yer mother never told ya it's rude ta gawk?"

"Yes, sir, she has."

"Well?"

The two of us were getting nowhere. It was time to be firm.

"Mr. Cornwall . . . about the money . . ."

"I told ya, son, there ain't no money. Ya tell yer Mr. Taylor I ain't got his three pound. He'll 'ave ta wait."

"Mr. Cornwall, I don't think ya understand."

With the heat of the oven in his face, Mr. Cornwall picked up a rolling pin and charged toward me. In seconds he was in front of me with his right arm raised high above his head. He was wild.

"Jaysus, lad. I can't pay the money if I ain't got it. I'm skint. D'ya hear me?"

"Dad!"

It was Alice, standing in the doorway behind me.

"Put it down, Dad."

Slowly Mr. Cornwall lowered his arm and dropped the rolling pin to the ground. I went to pick it up, but Alice stopped me.

"Just go," she said.

Before leaving, I turned at the doorway and saw father and daughter in each other's arms. Miraculously, words began to leave my mouth.

"Alice, I just wanted ta—"

"Leave us alone. Yer just like the rest of 'em."

As soon as my feet hit the footpath outside, my legs took me off at a cracking pace toward Richmond. Running had always come easy to me, but now as I double-timed it up Brunswick Street, each part of my body seemed intent on doing its own thing. There was no rhythm in my stride, and my breathing came loud and labored. So accustomed was I to the foulness of the Richmond air, it was as if my lungs wanted no part of the freshness the Fitzroy streets offered them.

The running, however, was the least of my problems. As I flew across Punt Road into Richmond, two names began filling my head—Alice and Kenneth Cornwall. With the Victoria Parade shops on either side of me, my mind returned to the cake shop in Fitzroy. My failure in retrieving Squizzy's money terrified me enough, what with the mood I'd left him in, but there was something else nagging me. It was the picture of Alice and her father in the back room. During the city runs, I'd been able to distance myself from Squizzy's debtors. To me they were simply names on a list.

But now, after my meeting with the Cornwalls, I realized that these people were more than just names. They were real people, desperate people—people with families, people just like Ma and me.

A little way up Church Street, outside an address well known to the men of Richmond, a familiar figure stepped from a gate and onto the path in front of me. It was Daisy Moloney. Had it been anyone else, I would have kept running. But Daisy Moloney was a good excuse for a walk.

"Afternoon, Daisy," I puffed, slowing up.

Seeing me, she broke into a smile.

"Charlie! Gawd, fer a minute there I thought ya was one a me customers. There's some right nutters among 'em."

"Ya knockin' off, are ya, Daisy?"

"That I am. Me youngest'll be wantin' some time on the breast, poor thing. 'Struth, they're fit ta burst, they are."

For a second I let my eyes drop to her chest and noticed a black silk camisole under her coat.

"I 'aven't seen ya fer a while, Charlie. Good Lord, yer a 'andsome devil. I tell ya, if ya was a bit older, I'd give up the game, I would. Ya'd put a smile on a lady's face, I'm sure a it. How's yer ma, by the way?"

"Not so good, as it 'appens. She's spendin' 'er days 'idin' in the 'ouse, cleanin'. No one comes visitin' no more. She's scared 'em all off. She reckons everyone's talkin' 'bout us."

"What about yer relations, Charlie? Surely there's someone who can help out?"

"Nah . . . Me dad's folks died when he was a lad, and Ma's . . . I dunno. They've never bothered with us, really."

Beside me, Daisy slipped her arm through mine.

"I'm sorry, Charlie," she said. "And what about you? How are ya, yerself?"

"I'm awright. I've found some work, as it 'appens."

"So I've 'eard, Charlie. They tell me yer runnin' fer Squizzy Taylor?"

"That's right."

"And what does yer ma think? I'm surprised she's agreed ta it."

Straightaway, Daisy read the answer in my face.

"Yer mean ta say she doesn't know? Good Lord, Charlie. What about yer wages, then? How are ya explainin' the money?"

"I'm not. I'm savin' it."

"But—"

"Don't worry, Daisy. We ain't starvin' yet. Ma don't discuss the finances with me, but I think we've a little in the purse still. I gotta do this while I can, though. It don't come 'round every day."

Daisy tightened her grip on my arm.

"Listen, Charlie," she said. "I know ya don't need me tellin' yer—after all, we all got ta make a livin'—but there's some nasty types in that Richmond push. Take it from me."

"I can look after meself, Daisy."

"I'm sure ya can, Charlie. Just watch yerself. Ya must be makin' a nice quid or two, eh?"

"He pays awright."

Before the incident with Mr. Peacock, I might well have left Daisy right then and headed to Darlington Parade, but the thought of her walking home alone unnerved me. With her good looks and smooth dark skin, she was a popular choice for the men who frequented her place of employ. And because she'd lost her husband in the war, many of those men believed they were entitled to a "free ride" after hours.

At number fifteen Cubitt Street, Daisy kissed my cheek and headed up the path. On the verandah she turned and waved.

"Ya use that money fer somethin' good, Charlie. Ya hear?"

As soon as she spoke, a baby began screaming inside. The door opened, and Daisy disappeared so quickly it was as if the house had swallowed her up. Although time was against me, I stood by her front gate awhile with her voice still ringing in my head.

Two words kept repeating themselves.

Something good . . .

Something good . . .

Something good . . .

My mind raced back to the cake shop, to Alice and her father, and suddenly I knew exactly what it was I had to do.

Quickly I raced home and let myself inside. In the living room Ma was curled up asleep on the floor with a scrubbing brush in her hand. Beside her a cake of soap sat floating in a bucket of murky water. I continued on to my room and dived under the bed in search of the envelope.

There.

Between thumb and forefinger, I counted three pound notes, folded them into my coat pocket with the rest of Squizzy's money, and headed out the door. This time the running came easy. By the time I'd reached the end of Cubitt Street, I'd settled into a rhythm so sweet I could have run a hundred miles.

Something good . . .

Something good . . .

Something good . . .

In a matter of minutes, Dolly was standing before me with a tumbler of whisky in her hand.

"Charlie, where've ya been?"

"I've been collectin' the money, just like Squizzy said."

"Ya better get in there. 'E's been callin' fer ya fer an hour."

After a few deep breaths, I made my way down the hall and poked my head through the office door. Seeing me, Squizzy shot up in his chair and went for a gun on the table in front of him.

"Flamin' 'eck, lad. What are ya thinkin', sneakin' up on a man like that? I've a good mind ta put a bullet in yer backside."

"I'm sorry, Mr. Taylor, I thought ya was in a meetin'."

Slowly Squizzy got up from his chair, moved to the window, and peeked through the curtain outside. When he returned, he dropped the gun onto the table, picked up his whisky, and drained it. His red cheeks told me it wasn't his first.

"Where ya been, anyway? Did ya stop off fer a picnic, lad?"

"No, sir."

"No? Ya took ya sweet time about it. D'ya 'ave the money?"

From my coat pocket I retrieved the notes and placed them on the table.

"Correct weight, is it, lad?"

"It's all there, Mr. Taylor."

"Very good."

In all my time working for Squizzy Taylor, I'd never seen him in such a state. As he moved to the window for another look outside, he reminded me of the rabbits down at Yarra Park. Even to be thinking such a thing was a dangerous occupation in itself, but to me, Squizzy Taylor looked scared.

At the window he spoke with his back to me.

"It's only fair ta warn ya, lad . . . things'll be heatin' up 'round 'ere. I've another liquor run fer ya in a couple a nights. It's a job fer two."

"We'll be 'ere, Mr. Taylor, no worries."

"Awright, Charlie. Get off 'ome."

CHAPTER FOURTEEN

That night, after dinner, I left Ma and Jack in front of the fire, loaded the trolley full of wood, and called on the Redmonds next door. It would take a lifetime to repay the Redmonds properly for all their kindness. But now, with a free hand at the wood yard, I was at least able to give them something. Out the back, Mrs. Redmond was hovering excitedly over a gramophone she had set up on a table on the verandah.

"Da-daaaah! . . . What d'ya think, Charlie?"

"'Struth, must've cost a fortune. Where'd ya get it?"

With a skipping rope draped over his shoulders, Mr. Redmond moved up beside me.

"It was the wife's idea, Charlie. I'm tellin' yer right now, I had nothin' ta do with it."

In these parts, a gramophone was as rare as hen's teeth, and quite frankly, I was a little surprised by Mr. Redmond's confession.

"What are ya talkin' about?" I said. "It's a beaut! You two'll be dancin' yer boots off."

Next to me, Mr. Redmond took a step back.

"Us two?" said his wife. "It's not fer us, Charlie. It's fer you."

"Me? What would I want with a gramophone?"

"Footwork, Charlie. It's ta help yer along with yer footwork."

Suddenly I understood the reason for Mr. Redmond's odd behavior.

If I'd needed any further reason to quit boxing, then this was it.

"Look, it's very kind of ya ta go ta all that bother," I said. "And it's not like I'm ungrateful or nothin', but I've got somethin' I need ta tell ya."

This time Mr. Redmond took a step forward.

"What is it, Charlie?"

"I'm retirin' from the boxin'."

"Ya what?"

"I'm retirin'."

"Retirin'? . . . It's the nursery rhymes, is it, lad?"

"Nah."

"It's the gramophone, then? I knew it were a daft idea."

"It's not the gramophone."

"But ya can't be retirin'. We haven't even started on the bag yet. Come on, we'll hit the bag."

"It's nothin' about the trainin', Mr. Redmond. I just ain't cut out fer the boxin', that's all. Runnin's me game."

For a few moments, the three of us stood quietly, surveying the training equipment. Finally, it was Mr. Redmond who broke the silence.

"Ya sure it weren't the gramophone?" he asked.

"I'm sure. But it does seem a bit of a waste. D'ya think I could borrow it fer a couple a nights, Mrs. Redmond? I've someone that needs a little cheerin' up."

"Course ya can, Charlie. Take it fer as long as ya like. There's a record there, too."

As was her habit of late, Mrs. Redmond raised her hand up to her mouth and half smiled before disappearing inside. It saddened me to see her behaving this way. Like Ma, she too had lost her smile. So conscious was she of her rotting teeth that now, whenever there was company about, she hid them behind her hand. And on those occasions when her hands were full and something tickled her fancy, she'd kill her smile by forcing her lips shut.

With her gone, Mr. Redmond and I began unloading the wood from my trolley. He too looked glum.

"Yer still runnin' fer Squizzy Taylor, I 'ear."

"I am, Mr. Redmond."

"Ya know, I 'eard a few things at the Bull and Mouth the other night, Charlie. They're sayin' there's an almighty stoush brewin' with the Fitzroy push. Guns an' all."

"I wouldn't know, Mr. Redmond. I keep me 'ead outta things like that. I'm runnin' is all."

"So ya keep sayin'."

The two of us continued on, then loaded the gramophone onto the empty trolley. Mr. Redmond seemed distracted.

"Ya know, I could train yer, if yer like," he said.

"Huh?"

"In the runnin', I mean."

"What makes yer think I need trainin'?"

"'Ave ya ever thought about racin', Charlie?"

"Racin'?"

"Yeah. There's a footrace I've been thinkin' of. Ya ever heard a the Ballarat Mile?"

"Can't say I 'ave."

"It's a professional race, with prize money an' all. I've seen yer runnin', Charlie. Yer a natural miler. With a bit a trainin', who knows?"

"Yer said there were prize money involved, Mr. Redmond?"

"That's right. There's a decent purse, from what I been told."

As I stood there in the Redmonds' yard, my thoughts returned once again to the cake shop. Suddenly Kenneth Cornwall appeared before me with the rolling pin raised high above his head. There was desperation in his eyes.

"And this Ballarat Mile, Mr. Redmond . . . It's ridgy-didge, is it?"

"Course it is, Charlie. We've a month or so ta get ready. I promise, there'll be no skippin'. It'll just be you and me. What d'ya say?"

"No skippin', eh?"

"Not even a hop."

I smiled and offered him my right hand.

"Awright, Mr. Redmond. Yer on."

At home I steered the squeaking trolley up the side of the house and out the back. Off to my right, near the fence, a bad-tempered ball of feathers jumped from his pen and craned his neck high.

'Struth!

Quickly I raised myself to match him and shouted, "I'm warnin' ya, Harry. Don't even think about it. How was I ta know ya were a boy?"

By the look of him, Harry didn't feel much like talking. Instead he raised the feathers on his back and charged, squawking and quacking so ferociously I very near soiled my pants.

The first nip caught my coat, so I hit back with my right hand and smacked his bill hard. With the determination of a bulldog, he came again, only this time he took a swipe between my legs.

"Ouch! That there were below the belt, Harry. If ya keep fightin' dirty, I'll 'ave ya."

I lashed out again with my right and smacked his bill for the second time. Neither of us was willing to back down, so the two of us went at it, trading blows for a while.

Nip.

Smack.

Nip.

Smack.

Nip.

Smack.

Finally I'd had enough. Next time he lunged, I took another swipe and caught him with an open hand. Then, before he had time to recover, I followed up with a backhander, so sweet it ruffled his feathers.

Finkin' and footwork.

He hadn't expected the one-two. As he waddled back, stunned, I opened the back door, picked up the gramophone, and slipped safely inside.

Had anyone been watching the bout, I have no doubt they would have awarded me the points. Still, you had to hand it to Harry—as a featherweight, he sure knew a thing or two about the fight game.

Inside, the house felt sleepy and warm. Ma and Jack were asleep in a living room chair, stretched contentedly in front of the fire like two cozy cats. I off-loaded the gramophone onto a side table and stood watching them awhile. I loved seeing them like this. Jack lay sprawled across Ma's chest, his head nestled in under her neck. Standing before them with my back to the fire, I was under no illusion as to who was responsible for my family's good fortune. It was Squizzy Taylor who was buttering our bread now, and for that I owed him a great deal.

Quietly, I lowered myself onto one knee and kissed Jack's cheek. He yawned, then wriggled onto his side. The movement seemed to trigger a response in Ma, who began patting his back gently with her right hand.

It was strange seeing Ma this close. For the last few weeks the two of us had pretty much kept our distance, but now, as my eyes examined her face, I felt a desperate need to touch her. With my forefinger, I gently brushed her dark fringe of hair from her eyes. Except for her eyelids and a set of tiny finger marks down her left cheek, her face was porcelain white. Cracks had begun to appear in the thick layers of powder around her mouth. I picked up her free hand and pressed her warm palm against my face. She stirred and opened her eyes.

"Charlie."

"It's awright, Ma."

"Who's 'ere? Don't tell me we've visitors callin'? Ya never told me we 'ad visitors."

"It's just me, Ma. Everythin's awright. Here, let me take Jack. I'll put 'im in the bassinet."

In the past, the slightest disturbance would have woken Jack, but now as I lifted him up, his body fell heavy and limp across my shoulder. The warmth in the house agreed with him so much that he'd taken to sleeping through the night. The serenity had unnerved me at first. More than once I'd found myself tiptoeing down the hall to Ma's room to check on the rise and fall of his chest.

With Jack tucked safely in the bassinet, I returned to the living room with two cups of steaming tea. Ma was sitting up, staring into the fire.

"He's put on a few pounds, I reckon, Ma."

"That 'e 'as, Charlie. He's an appetite on 'im, fer sure."

On the rare occasions the two of us spent time together, the conversation always revolved around Jack.

Jack was easy.

It made a change from the time my dad had been alive. Whenever the family sat down for dinner, Ma would be at me, firing questions across the table.

Crikey, dear, yer as bad as a copper, my father would joke. Then he'd turn to me and wink. *If I was you, Charlie, I'd be careful answerin' any of 'er questions. Ya'll get yerself inta strife.*

But things had changed. Now Ma refrained from even the simplest of questions. She never asked me about my schooling anymore, nor did she inquire after my friends. Questions involved answers, and for Ma, I suppose, it was easier not to ask. So instead, the two of us made do with nappy rash and rice pudding.

Draining the last of my tea, I suddenly remembered the gramophone.

"I nearly forgot, Ma," I said, rising to my feet. "I've a little surprise fer ya. . . . What d'ya think?"

"A gramophone? But, Charlie, where did ya—"

"Don't worry, Ma, I borrowed it from the Redmonds. I've a record 'ere as well. What d'ya say?"

"I don't know, Charlie. I'm not ready ta be—"

"Ma, if I 'ave to hear another word about the chafin' on Jack's arse, I reckon I'll go mad. Come on, why don't ya get rid a yer apron?"

If there was one thing my parents had loved to do, it was dance. Before Jack was born and when the money permitted, the two of them would leave me at home with the Redmonds and head off to one of the many dance halls in town. Nothing had pleased me more than to hear them return home from a night of dancing. They'd burst through the front door, kissing and cuddling like a couple half their age. Sometimes my father would stumble into my room and sit himself on the edge of my bed.

Charlie, he'd whisper. *Whatever ya do . . . find yerself a girl who can dance.*

I cranked the gramophone, then gently lowered the needle into place.

"Ya'll like this one, Ma. It's called 'I'm Forever Blowin' Bubbles.'"

As I stepped to the center of the room, Ma rose from her chair and slowly removed her apron. She was stalling. She forced a smile, then backpedaled to the fire. As a piano started up, I went to her and extended my hand.

"May I 'ave this dance?" I asked.

Finally she surrendered and took my hand.

Only a few steps in, I discovered that dancing was a great deal harder than it looked. My parents had made it seem easy, the way they glided across the floor.

"There's a bit to this dancin' caper, Ma. How am I doin'?"

"Yer doin' fine, Charlie. Stop lookin' at yer feet and relax a little."

Her voice sounded strange, so I looked up at her face and noticed she was smiling.

"Yer not laughin' at me dancin', are ya, Ma?"

"Laughin'? Me?"

"Yeah, you. Looked as though ya were laughin'."

When the record finished, I replaced the needle and quickly returned to Ma. I snapped my fingers and hummed the tune out loud.

"By crikey, Charlie, yer gettin' more like yer father every day."

I smiled and kept snapping until Ma pulled me close.

"They never liked 'im, ya know, Charlie."

Her words took me by surprise.

"Who didn't, Ma?" I asked, confused.

"My parents," she replied. "Yer grandma and grandpa . . . They disapproved of 'im. Can ya believe that, Charlie? They wanted nothin' ta do with me after I married yer father. Said I was marryin' below meself."

"Is that why they never come ta see us, then?"

"Yeah, that's why, Charlie. . . . Silly, ain't it?"

"Are ya sorry? Are ya, Ma?"

"Sorry? Don't be daft. Why would I be sorry? I got you and Jack, 'aven't I?"

"Yeah, course ya 'ave, Ma. I ain't goin' nowhere."

As she wrapped her arms around my back, I felt her head fall onto my shoulder.

"I miss him, Charlie," she whispered.

"Me too, Ma. Me too."

CHAPTER FIFTEEN

The next morning, as I closed our front door, I filled my head with Ma's smiling face. Mr. Redmond was standing on his verandah checking the conditions overhead. He appeared to be talking to himself, but then I noticed Clarrie's head poking from the Gladstone bag he had slung over his left shoulder.

"Awright, smartarse, yer on," he said. "I'll bet ya a bone it starts rainin' while we're out."

Seeing me, he stepped off the verandah, then gave Clarrie's head a pat.

"Here's our man now, Clarrie. . . . Charlie, I'd like ya ta meet yer new trainin' partner."

"Who, 'im?"

"Too right. The idea came ta me last night. Any mug can run a mile, Charlie. What ya need is a sprint. Ya need ta be able ta pull out somethin' in the 'ome straight."

As we continued on, Bert Robinson announced his arrival in Cubitt Street.

"Milko!" he cried. "Milko!"

Outside number twenty-four, he pulled on the reins, and his aging Clydesdale came to a halt.

"Milko! . . . Milko!"

From the safety of the Gladstone bag, Clarrie pricked his ears and began barking.

"Mornin', Bert," called Mr. Redmond.

"Mornin', Cecil."

Like most of the people in Cubitt Street, Bert Robinson was all too familiar with Mr. Redmond's fixation with the elements. He looked skyward, then shook his head.

"There's a spot a rain comin', I reckon, Cecil."

"Rain? Yer've got ta be kiddin'. Ain't one of them clouds is a cumulus. What yer seein' is more ya cirrus variety."

"Yer seem mighty sure a yerself, Cecil. Ya willin' ta make it interestin'?"

Mr. Redmond turned to me and winked.

"Very well, Bert. . . . Same deal as last time?"

"Sounds fair. If it rains before lunch, though, even a spot, I'll be expectin' some rabbits."

"Ha! Yer outta ya depth, I'm afraid, Bert. Ya may as well pour me a couple a pints a milk now, and I'll take 'em 'ome ta the missus."

By the time we arrived at Yarra Park, Clarrie was itching to go. As I sat on the ground tying the laces on my boots, Mr. Redmond plucked Clarrie from the bag and held him tight.

"Now remember what I said, Charlie. Fer a mile race, ya need some speed in yer legs. Ya'll 'ave ya work cut out fer ya, but I want ya ta stay with 'im as best ya can. Awright?"

I nodded. "Awright."

"Come on, then, on yer feet."

As I stretched my legs, Mr. Redmond gave Clarrie a final kiss, then leaned toward me.

"By the way, I'd prefer ya left the rabbitin' ta Clarrie, if ya don't mind. People might start talkin' if they spot ya with a rabbit in yer mouth. . . . Awright, are ya ready?"

I was.

Mr. Redmond kept a tight hold on Clarrie, then lowered him to the ground.

"Take yer marks . . . set . . . go!"

We were off.

In a matter of seconds, Clarrie had opened up a sizeable gap. He tore across the park and headed in a straight line toward the river, then disappeared into some bushes.

Mr. Redmond shouted instructions behind me.

"Stay with 'im, Charlie!"

When I arrived at the bushes, Clarrie emerged, wild with excitement. He stood for a moment, panting, then hurled himself into the undergrowth again. Suddenly a rabbit darted out some five yards to my left, with Clarrie close behind. From a standing start I worked my arms and sped off after them. My goal now was to keep them in sight.

Sensing that Clarrie was closing, the rabbit began changing its line. It darted left, then right, causing me to slip.

"What are ya restin' fer?" screamed Mr. Redmond. "Get up, Charlie!"

Quickly I picked myself up and saw that the rabbit was heading back to the bushes. Just as it looked as if he'd made it, Clarrie pounced.

In a final desperate bid, the rabbit rolled onto its back and began thrashing its back legs into Clarrie's ribs. Too late. Clarrie lunged, opened his mouth, and sank his teeth into the rabbit's neck.

The bunny was stew.

. . .

Six rabbits later, Mr. Redmond blew a whistle, calling it quits.

"Awright, you two," he shouted. "That'll do ya fer today."

Exhausted, I ambled back across the park, sucking in lung-fuls of air. At my feet, Clarrie looked disappointed.

"Good work, Charlie," said a smiling Mr. Redmond. "How are ya feelin'?"

I collapsed at his feet, barely able to speak.

"Flamin' 'eck," I gasped. "I ain't run as 'ard as that in me life."

"Ya did well, Charlie, real well. Ya'll be flyin' before long. Take it from me."

Lying on my back, I looked up at the sky as a drop of rain hit my face.

"I ain't no expert, Mr. Redmond, but them clouds up there . . . ain't they cumulus?"

Strangely enough, when I met Nostrils at the corner of Swan and Church streets that night, I was in the mood for dancing. Things were finally looking up. As I approached the intersection, Nostrils stepped from under a shop awning and waved.

"How's it goin', Charlie?"

"I'm scrapin' by, Nostrils. What about yerself? How's the trainin' goin?"

"Couldn't be better. They've picked me at center 'alf forward tomorra."

"Center 'alf forward? About time, I reckon. Ya were wasted out on the flank. Key position, that's yer go. Who've ya got, anyway?"

"Carlton. They're bottom a the ladder."

"Flamin' 'eck, ya'll kick a bagful."

Talented as he was, Nostrils had never been big on compliments. After only a few games, the name Norman Heath was already doing the rounds amongst the people of Richmond as a junior who would one day wear the yellow and black at senior level. Had it been me in his shoes, I daresay the attention would have caused my head to swell the size of a football. But Nostrils wasn't like that. On the football field, he was as ferocious as anyone I'd seen. You could see it in his eyes. He wanted nothing more than to one day fill a spot in the seniors, but come siren time, when he stripped the jumper from his back, Nostrils could not understand what all the fuss was about.

Chatting away, the two of us set off up Church Street toward Squizzy's place.

"How's the boxin' goin', Charlie?" he asked.

"I've retired."

"Ya what?"

"I've hung up me gloves, Nostrils."

"Dead set?"

"Yeah. Mr. Redmond's trainin' me fer a footrace. I'm enterin' the Ballarat Mile. Ya heard a it?"

"Nah, I can't say I 'ave."

"There's prize money an' all."

As we walked up Church Street, I noticed a FOR SALE sign hanging on the fence of Porter's Wood Yard. Nostrils pulled up beside me.

"Well, fancy that," I said. "Mr. Porter is sellin' the wood yard. Imagine ownin' a wood yard, Nostrils."

Nostrils laughed, then moved in front of the sign as if posing for a photograph.

"I can see it now, Charlie." He smiled. "The Heath and Feehan Timber Company. It's got a ring about it, I reckon."

"'Ang on a jiff. Yer takin' a few liberties there, ain't ya? Yer've given yerself top billin'. Feehan and Heath, if ya don't mind."

As we pressed on, the debate continued until we turned into Darlington Parade. Besides Squizzy's Buick, two other cars were parked outside number eighteen. With Nostrils behind me, I pushed through the front gate and noticed three bicycles leaning against the side fence.

"Squizzy 'avin' a party, is he?" asked Nostrils.

"Not likely," I replied. "He's in no mood ta be celebratin', I'll give yer the nod. Best if ya let me do the talkin' tonight, Nostrils."

Judging from the transport out front, I knew there to be a fair crowd gathered inside. Something was up.

As we stepped onto the verandah, Nostrils pointed to a metal panel newly installed at eye level in the front door.

"What's goin' on?" he whispered.

I shrugged and rapped my knuckles on the wood below.

Seconds later the panel slid open and we were greeted by a pair of steely dark eyes. It was Knuckles.

"Yeah?"

"It's Charlie Feehan, Knuckles. Mr. Taylor's expectin' us."

Inside, a haze of cigarette smoke hung thick in the air. In his office, Squizzy had the floor.

"It's all set, then. Tomorra night we take it to 'em. Dasher and Fred, ya'll be drivin' the cars. I want three men in each. When we pull up outside, I want yas all ta empty yer guns inta the 'ouse. Aim fer the windows, and if ya see anythin' move inside, shoot ta kill. A few minutes is all we'll 'ave, gents. Any questions?"

There were none.

"Awright, then, see yas tomorra. And there'll be no drinkin' beforehand. I want keen eyes on the lot a ya."

Standing with my back hard against the wall, I counted eight men file past me out the door. When the last of them was gone, Squizzy appeared in the hallway with a gun in his hand.

"Well, well, well. If it ain't the Good Samaritan 'imself. Come down 'ere, lad. I want a word with ya."

During my time under Squizzy's employ, I'd seen my boss in many different moods. I'd grown accustomed to his sarcastic tongue. But tonight the tone in his voice was different. There was a viciousness in it, and it frightened me.

I shuffled down the hall and stepped into Squizzy's office.

"What the flamin' 'eck d'ya think yer up ta?" he roared. "Ya thinkin' a joinin' the priesthood, are ya, lad? It's charity work yer interested in, is it?"

The outburst forced me back a step.

"I'm sorry, Mr. Taylor, I don't think I follow."

"Yer don't, eh? Well, let me fill ya in, then. Yesterday, I had a visit from yer Kenneth Cornwall, as it 'appens. Yer familiar with the man, are ya not?"

"Yes, sir. He runs the cake shop in Fitzroy."

"That's right. Well, this mug turns up at me house, pleadin' fer some extra time on his payment. Anyway, I take a look at the books, and what d'ya know? Seems this Cornwall bloke's already paid up."

"Mr. Taylor, I can explain. . . ."

In a flash, Squizzy jumped to his feet, gun in hand. He rushed at me and stopped only a few inches from my face. I did not meet his eyes at first. I looked slightly down and saw that one of the veins in his neck had swelled to the size of a sausage.

"I don't want ya ta explain nothin', ya little runt. I'm not payin' ya ta be givin' me money away. I'm conductin' a business 'ere. 'Struth, if anyone gets wind a this, I'll have every no-'oper in Melbourne lined up at me door wantin' a 'andout."

I stood before him, shaking, resisting the urge to wipe his spit from my face. Suddenly his eyes left me and settled on Nostrils.

"And what about you, nosy? Did ya 'ave anythin' ta do with this?"

"Er . . ."

"He 'ad nothin' ta do with it, Mr. Taylor. It were me."

Just as quickly as it had come, the bulging vein in his neck disappeared. It was as if someone had pricked it with a fork. After a couple of deep breaths, he replaced the gun in his hand with a piece of paper from the table.

"I've got a liquor run 'ere that'll be right up yer alley, lad. Fitzroy, as it 'appens."

He threw the paper to me. It dropped short and fell to the floor in front of the desk.

"I tell ya what . . . if ya stuff this up, ya can find yerself another job."

I'd reached the door with the paper in my hand when Squizzy's voice stopped me.

"By the way, lad—and ya can take this from me—it ain't a good time ta be makin' friends in Fitzroy."

· · ·

Outside in Darlington Parade, I was still shaking. It wasn't until we got to the end of the street that one of us found the courage to speak.

It was Nostrils.

He looked over his shoulder just in case.

"He's lost 'is marbles, Charlie. This is gettin' dangerous."

In my heart I knew he was right, but it was my head I was listening to. Ma and Jack were in there, cuddling in front of the fire.

"Ya can call it quits if ya like, Nostrils," I said, walking on. "I'll do the job on me own."

Nostrils quickened his pace and grabbed hold of my arm.

"Charlie, will ya listen ta me? I'm yer mate. Someone's gunna get 'imself killed 'ere. Did ya not 'ear 'im? 'E's talkin' guns?"

"I 'eard 'im, Nostrils, and I ain't stoppin'. If it weren't fer Squizzy Taylor, we'd be out on the street. Yer fergettin', I ain't got a father like yerself. I wish I did, but I ain't. And it's not as if me ma can go out ta work. She's got Jack on the breast. It's me who's gotta think about the family now. We ain't got any money comin' in. This is all we got. If yer want ta quit, it's up ta you. I can do it on me own."

With that, I left Nostrils and turned the corner into Waltham Street. As I pulled the piece of paper from my coat pocket, I heard footsteps behind me. They grew louder and louder until Nostrils was at my side again, smiling.

"I'm only doin' it 'cause I know yer afraid a the dark," he said. "Anyway, yer too scrawny ta be luggin' liquor by yerself."

"Thanks, Nostrils."

By the time we got to Goodwood Street, the two of us were laughing. At Henry Stokes' two-up school we made our way down the side and around to the rear door. Rubbing his hands together, Nostrils stepped forward as if he was taking center stage at Her Majesty's Theatre itself. Then, with a dramatic sweep of his arm, he rang the bell.

Ding! Ding! . . . Ding! Ding!

"Not bad, eh?" he asked.

"Yer a natural, Nostrils. And 'ere's me believin' I could 'ave done the job without yer. I dunno what I were thinkin'."

On the other side of the door came the sound of movement.

"Identify yerselves!" called a familiar voice.

Nostrils, still buoyed by his stunning performance with the bell, stepped forward and yelled a reply.

"It's Squizzy Taylor's lads, Mr. Jenkins."

Seconds later the door opened and Jenkins ushered us in.

"Security, lads," he explained. "Boss's orders. It's all ready fer ya. Let's see . . . three whisky and a dozen beer. It's a load and a 'alf tonight. Is it far ya gotta go?"

"It is, sir," I replied. "All the way ta Fitzroy."

"'Struth. Wait on, I'll see if there's a trolley floatin' around."

From a darkened doorway, Jenkins steered a flat-top trolley toward us. He was an old man, too old to be sorting bottles, and when he pulled up beside us he took a few moments to catch his breath.

"We'll be right loadin' up," I said. "Why don't yer take a seat?"

"Thanks, lads. Don't mind if I do. They'll be puttin' me out ta pasture before long."

First, Nostrils and I divided the bottles into three cement bags, then lifted them carefully onto the trolley. To hide the liquor, we smashed up boxes with our boots and placed the broken wood over the load. When we were ready, Jenkins lifted himself from the chair and bade us farewell.

"Now, lads," he said, "ya'll stick out like dogs' balls wheelin' that thing around at this time a night. Yer best ta take the back streets where ya can."

"Awright, Mr. Jenkins, we'll keep it in mind."

Even without a trolley, running liquor was fraught with danger. It was the weight of the load that was the problem. In a footrace, I'd back Nostrils and me against a copper any day, but with the three bags of bottles in our possession, the two of us were sitting ducks. And it wasn't just the law you had to look out for. In these parts, there were men so thirsty for the grog I had no doubt that some of them would have gone the knuckle for a half bottle of stale beer.

At the end of Goodwood Street, Nostrils and I slowed to a halt. He looked nervous.

"What d'ya reckon, Charlie?"

"We'll be right, Nostrils. The drop-off's in Gore Street. We ain't got much choice but ta take a few main roads early on. After that, we'll cut through the gardens in Fitzroy, and we're 'ome. Sound awright?"

"Yeah, but I reckon we need ta sort somethin' out before we start."

"What's that, Nostrils?"

"Which dog ball d'ya wanna be, left or right?"

CHAPTER SIXTEEN

While covering the main roads, we decided that Nostrils would walk twenty yards ahead, checking for trouble as we went. If the path looked clear, then he'd wave me on. Surprisingly, we made our way up Punt Road and Wellington Parade without incident, then steered the trolley into the darkness of the Fitzroy Gardens.

Easy.

Although the going was slow, we left the main path and opted for the grass, dragging the trolley behind us. At first, everything appeared black, but once our eyes adjusted we noticed how well the gardens were lit.

"'Struth," whispered Nostrils, "it's like Bourke Street in 'ere."

Despite the full moon overhead, the gardens were still a better option than the streets. In the open spaces we moved fast, stopping to rest in the shadows thrown by the giant elm trees. By the time we reached the Albert Road border, we were exhausted.

For a few minutes the two of us stood close, gazing up along the road ahead.

"We're nearly there, Nostrils. What say we knock this on the 'ead?"

"Suits me. I'll be needin' a decent nap before the game tomorra."

"Awright, then. Just like before. You go on ahead, and remember—keep yer wits about ya."

About twenty yards up Eades Street, Nostrils turned and waved me on.

When I pushed the trolley forward, it rolled so smoothly across the footpath it was as if the thing was driving itself. With St. John's Cathedral on my left, I continued on and stopped at Victoria Parade.

This was it—the home straight.

The finishing line, Gore Street, was in sight. We had only to cross to the other side and we were there.

Out on the tram tracks, Nostrils gave me a wave.

Although there were people about, we had to keep moving.

As gently as I could, I rolled the trolley off the footpath onto Victoria Parade and sped forward. The timing could not have been better. Nostrils met me on the other side, and after a short distance the two of us swung left into Gore Street.

"We're lookin' for number nine, Nostrils," I said, relieved. "A Mr. Wheeler."

Beside me Nostrils counted the numbers out loud.

"Three . . . five . . . seven . . . nine. This is it, Charlie. Number nine Gore Street."

As we pushed through the gate, the two of us relaxed a little and managed a smile.

"I tell ya what, Charlie," said Nostrils. "There's gotta be easier ways a makin' a quid."

"Maybe." I smirked at him. "But think a all the fun yer 'avin'."

Number nine Gore Street was a single-fronted dwelling in a sad state of disrepair. So bad was its condition, I had to double-check the address just to make sure we had it right.

"What's yer problem?" asked Nostrils.

"Nothin'. Just seems a bit strange we'd be deliverin' so much liquor ta a place like this."

"What's it say on yer paper?"

"Mr. Wheeler. Nine Gore Street, Fitzroy."

"Nine it is, then. C'mon, Charlie, let's get this done. I need me beauty sleep."

Stuffing the paper into my pocket, I left Nostrils on the path, stepped up to the door, and knocked.

Nothing.

Behind me Nostrils began fidgeting.

"Put some bloody effort into it, ya sheila."

I was about to try again when the door clicked open a fraction.

"Mr. Wheeler?" I asked.

"Who wants ta know?"

"We're Mr. Taylor's lads, sir. Here with the refreshments."

"Leave 'em on the porch."

"But—"

"Leave 'em on the porch, I say. And don't think I won't be watchin'."

Strange as it was, Nostrils and I had little choice but to do as we were told. We off-loaded the liquor and, without so much as a thank-you, found ourselves steering the empty trolley back down Gore Street, toward home.

As we crossed over Victoria Parade, a wave of relief flooded through us.

"I don't know what ya were worryin' about, Nostrils," I joked. "Yer like an old boiler, the way ya carry on sometimes."

"Me?"

"Yeah, you. Listen, d'ya fancy a nice stroll in the gardens?"

"As a matter a fact, I do. Only don't go gettin' any ideas."

"Ideas? Flamin' 'eck, yer got tickets on yerself? There ain't no amount a beauty sleep goin' ta improve that melon a yers, trust me."

The journey home through the gardens was mostly downhill, so Nostrils, like the Prince of Wales himself, boarded the trolley and demanded a ride.

"Take me 'ome, Charlie boy, and don't spare the 'orses."

In seconds the two of us were hurtling down the path, howling up at the moon like a couple of wild dogs. As we careened toward a bend in the path, I noticed a group of boys gathered near an elm trunk farther up on our right. Quickly I dropped my boots to the ground in an effort to slow the trolley, but it was too late. Six boys stepped out onto the path in front of us. At the head of them stood Jimmy Barlow.

Six against two. The odds were against us again.

Standing some ten yards away, Barlow took a swig from a bottle of beer, then handed it to one of his mates.

"Ain't it funny, fellas, the people ya bump inta in the gardens? Are yas lookin' fer a good time, ladies?"

Nostrils joined me at the head of the trolley.

"Not tonight, thanks, Jimmy," he replied. "But I was wonderin' if I could trouble ya fer a couple a tips."

Quickly I leaned over and whispered a warning. "Pull yer head in, Nostrils."

Not surprisingly, he ignored me.

"It's the footy," he continued. "I don't seem ta be gettin' me 'ands on the ball these days."

To my way of thinking, there's a time and a place for taking the mickey—and quite clearly this was not one of them. Had I not been able to see Nostrils' moonlit beak from the corner of my left eye, I would have sworn I was standing next to Squizzy Taylor himself.

As I knew he would, Barlow charged, only this time the others came with him. We hadn't the distance between us like in our last encounter in the park, but we had the trolley. With all my might, I pushed it forward to slow them, and ran. It all happened so quickly. Together, Nostrils and I jumped from the blocks. One second he was beside me, the next he was down. He'd slipped.

In every person's life, there come moments that define who you are—minuscule moments where you're called upon to act, faster than a flip of a coin.

Heads or tails.

Yes or no.

Go or stay.

Perhaps my mind was already made up, but as I turned and saw them on top of him, Nostrils raised his head and screamed.

"Run, Charlie! Run!"

After only a short distance the two who were after me gave up the chase. Even still, I continued running, left then right, darting behind trees until I arrived at the Albert Road border. It was a mistake to be out in the open, so I walked back into the gardens and rested in some bushes. My chest was heaving.

Should I return to Nostrils or go for help?

He was my best friend. I couldn't leave him.

After a few minutes I left the safety of the bushes and headed along the west side of the gardens, with Lansdowne Street on my right. Somewhere near the middle, I swung left and inward, toward the main path.

In the open spaces, like before, I traveled quickly, then propped myself beside a tree while contemplating my next move.

Soon enough I heard voices. It was amazing how well they carried in the night. They were coming from my right, some thirty yards, at a guess. At first the voices were nothing more than murmurs, but as I wriggled forward on my belly, I was able to hear their words as clear as if I was standing next to them. Some fifteen yards away I was now, close enough to see their moonlit faces.

Nostrils was on the ground with Barlow beside him.

"And when ya get the ball," Barlow said, "it's a piece a cake . . . all ya gotta do is kick it."

Winding up, he slammed his right boot into Nostrils' ribs.

"Are ya gettin' the 'ang a it yet?"

Nostrils moaned and grabbed at his side.

"Pick 'im up, fellas. I'm gunna teach 'im a lesson. I don't reckon 'e'll be fergettin' this one in a while."

Once Nostrils was on his feet, Barlow positioned himself in front of him, only inches from his face.

"Now, this 'ere is lesson number two. When playin' from behind, yer've gotta remember ta punch."

A devastating right cross connected with Nostrils' jaw.

Crack!

Instantly, Nostrils' feet gave way and he dropped to the ground.

"Pick 'im up!" Barlow barked. "Ya know, this is fun," he continued. "Maybe I orta take up teachin' full-time."

Gallantly, Nostrils raised his head, then spat a wad of blood into the face in front of him.

"Yer fergettin' one thing, Jimmy," Nostrils slurred through a swollen lip. "Yer gotta be able ta read if yer thinkin' a teachin'."

Barlow took a step back and wiped his face clean.

"I see we got a troublemaker in the class, fellas," he said. "Disruptin' all the others who are tryin' ta learn. Put 'im on the trolley. I think it's about time we learned 'im some manners."

Suddenly I wished I'd gone for help. Lying there in the wet grass, I told myself over and over to move, but it was as if my body was frozen stiff.

While Nostrils lay unmoving on the trolley, Barlow produced something from inside his coat. The object was long and slender, maybe two feet in length.

"I think yer gunna like me little friend 'ere. I've gotta warn ya, though, he don't play fair, like me."

Nostrils made a pathetic attempt to break free.

"Hold 'im down, fellas," ordered Barlow. "I'm gunna knee-cap the bludger."

Paralyzed with fear, my body refused to budge.

I had to do something.

For Christ's sake, move!

Slowly Barlow moved into position next to the trolley.

He took up a stance, left foot forward, then raised the bar above his head.

Move, ya sack a shit! Move!

Heads or tails.

Yes or no.

Go or stay.

As Barlow slammed the bar down onto my best friend's knee, I buried my face in the grass and screamed.

"No! . . ."

How long I lay there, I don't know, but when I raised my head they were gone. Only Nostrils remained.

Again I attempted to lift myself up, but still my limbs refused to budge.

Far worse than fear, it was shame that paralyzed me now.

How could I face him?

"Charlie!"

The sound of Nostrils' voice startled me.

"Charlie?"

"Over 'ere, Nostrils. I'm on me way."

It was too late for heroics.

At the main path, I leaned over the trolley and saw a trickle of blood coming from the corner of Nostrils' mouth. Through gritted teeth he sucked in breaths, short and sharp. Then, feeling my hands on his shoulder, he opened his eyes and coughed.

Pink foam bubbled from his mouth.

"Don't worry . . . Charlie."

He was panting now.

"I showed 'em . . . a thing . . . or two. . . . They won't . . . be . . . botherin' . . . us . . . fer . . . a while."

"Stop jokin' fer a second, will ya? Are ya bad?"

"It's bad . . . Charlie. . . . I think . . . they . . . busted . . . me knee . . . and . . . me ribs. . . . I can't . . . breathe. . . ."

"Nostrils! Stay with me!"

He was fading, fast.

Quickly, I turned the trolley around, bent low, and pushed.

"Nostrils!"

Left, right, left, right, left, right.

The tiny bubbles around his mouth, although they frightened me, seemed to give me strength. I imagined myself as strong as ten men. I locked my arms and heaved.

"Hang on, Nostrils, we're nearly there."

Out on the streets I straightened my back a little and gathered speed. Wherever possible, corners were to be avoided, so I opted for the most direct route. From Albert Road I turned right into Gisborne Street, with the Eastern Hill Fire Station on my left.

This was the moment I'd been dreading—Victoria Parade.

"I'm sorry, Nostrils," I hollered, "but this is gunna hurt."

As we rattled across the tram tracks, a strangled groan was forced from his lips.

Without stopping, I continued on and steered Nostrils toward St. Vincent's Hospital. The timing could not have been better. Just as the two of us arrived out front, a nurse in a crisp white uniform pushed through the front door.

"If ya don't mind, Sister," I yelled. "Comin' through."

Written in big red letters above the front desk was the word CASUALTY. For some reason I'd expected a group of doctors at the ready, but the only people about were patients, sitting off to my right, nursing various injuries.

I hadn't come all this way to wait in a line. Nostrils needed attention.

Steering the trolley to the center of the room, I filled my lungs and screamed.

"*Casualty!*"

In seconds a doctor and nurse burst through the double doors in front of me, looking none too pleased.

"What's the meaning of—"

Surveying the scene, the doctor seemed to swallow his words. He dropped to his knees and pressed a stethoscope to Nostrils' chest.

"What happened?"

"We got rolled. It's 'is ribs and 'is left knee."

"How long has he been like this, lad?"

"A few minutes," I replied. "Maybe ten. He'll be awright, won't 'e?"

"We'll do our best. You wait here, lad. I'll be wanting a word with you. Get him into theater, Nurse, and call for Dr. Flannigan."

As I sat there surrounded by white walls and hospital smells, it reminded me of the time my father had been sick. It was the waiting that was the worst.

Maybe two hours had passed before a copper strolled in and approached the nurse at the front desk. After they'd spoken for a while, she pointed my way, and the copper nodded.

I hadn't expected the law.

"I understand yer the fella who brought in the young lad on a trolley?" he asked.

"I am, Constable."

"I'd like a word with ya, then."

The copper craned his neck toward a couple of chairs off to our right. Once we were seated, he produced a notebook and the interview began.

"Name?"

"Charlie Feehan."

"Address?"

"Fifteen Cubitt Street, Richmond."

"Yer a long way from 'ome, lad. What brings ya out at this time a night?"

"Lookin' fer scraps, we were, Constable. That's why we 'ad the trolley with us."

His eyes left the notebook and settled on my face.

"Scraps, ya say? In Fitzroy?"

"That's right. Wood, metal, bottles—anythin' worth a quid."

"I see. And ya say ya were rolled, is that right?"

"Yes, sir. In the gardens, just down the road."

"And what was it ya were lookin' fer in the gardens? Collectin' bird shit, were ya, lad?"

The question caught me off guard.

"Shortcut, sir."

Resting back in his chair, the constable eyed me suspiciously, then smiled.

"And I understand it's yer mate on the table in there? Is that right?"

"Yes."

"You'll 'ave ta forgive me, but I'm a bit slow on the uptake sometimes. Can ya tell me somethin', then?"

The smirk on his face told me he was beginning to enjoy it.

"From what I been told," he continued, "the fella ya brought in is in a pretty bad way. How come yer sittin' 'ere, without a scratch? It don't seem ta add up, what with the two of ya bein' best mates an' all."

Explaining myself to a mustache-twirling copper was the last thing I felt like doing.

"It 'appened so quickly," I told him. "It was dark. When we

spotted the others, the two of us took off, and I kept runnin'. When I came back, it were too late."

"So ya saw the others, then? How many did ya count?"

"Six."

"Six? Are ya familiar with any of 'em?"

"Like I said, Constable—it were dark."

"It's a serious complaint yer makin', lad."

"I think yer mistaken, sir. Ya'd better check them notes. I never made a complaint. I only brought me mate in fer attention."

Just then the doctor appeared from behind the double doors.

"How is 'e, Doctor?" I asked, jumping from my chair. "He'll be awright, won't 'e?"

"He's going to be sore for quite a while, but he'll be all right. He's as strong as an ox. You must be Charlie, are you, lad?"

"Yes, Doctor."

"He was asking for you before he went under. I'll need to contact his parents. Do you know the address, Charlie?"

"Yes, sir."

"Right, then. I take it you've finished with the lad, Constable? Come this way, Charlie."

CHAPTER SEVENTEEN

After everything that had happened, I could not bring myself to face Mr. and Mrs. Heath. I'd told enough lies for one night.

So after I'd given the doctor Nostrils' address, I left the hospital, scratch-free, and headed toward Richmond. Walking the deserted streets alone, I was soon overcome by violent waves of nausea. As a horrible burning sensation rose up into my throat, I searched for a lamppost, grabbed hold of it, and spewed a foul yellow mixture into the gutter.

It was after midnight by the time I arrived home. Exhausted, I kicked off my boots and slipped quietly into bed.

The next morning appeared, at first, no different from any other. I rolled onto my side and saw a young man in the mold on my wall, his left leg severed above the knee.

Nostrils!

Slowly the pieces from last night began to fall into place.

Today was Saturday, and Nostrils, Richmond Hill's new center half forward, would not be taking the field.

Hearing the sound of laughter, I slipped out of bed, picked up my boots, and made my way to the kitchen. At the table, Ma was busy feeding Jack some bread and jam.

"Ma?"

I was stunned.

Seeing her face, powder-free, I let the boots slip from my hand and fall to the ground with a thud.

"I scrub up awright fer an old boiler, don't ya reckon?"

Speechless, I stood for a while staring back at her rosy red cheeks.

"Is it really you, Ma?"

"Course it's me, Charlie. Who were ya expectin' ta be sittin' down fer breakfast, Dame Nellie Melba?"

"Ya look beautiful, Ma. Really beautiful."

"Thank you, Charlie."

With Jack in her arms, she rose from her chair, took a piece of bread, and popped it into my mouth.

"Hang on a jiff," I protested. "Where are ya goin'? I ain't finished lookin'."

"Come with me, Charlie," she replied. "There's somethin' I want ya ta see."

As we made our way to the yard, Harry jumped from his pen, ready for round two. When he saw that Ma was with me, he slowed to a waddle and brushed himself against her leg.

"What is it ya want ta show me, Ma?" I asked.

"I've been waitin' all mornin' fer this." She smiled. "Here, 'ang on ta Jack fer a bit."

After handing me Jack, she turned, then picked up the tin of white powder she'd left sitting beside the back door.

"I don't reckon I'll be needin' this anymore," she said, removing the lid.

Ceremoniously, she held the tin aloft, walked over to the dam, and emptied it in.

"There ya go, Harry, me luv. It's all yers."

CHAPTER EIGHTEEN

Back at Cubitt Street after another training session at Yarra Park, I said goodbye to Mr. Redmond and made my way through our front gate. The sweet sound of music was playing inside.

"I'm 'ome, Ma," I yelled, pushing through the door. "Got a couple a rabbits fer ya."

"In 'ere, Charlie. We've a visitor."

The face that greeted me in the living room, dare I say it, was even more beautiful than my ma's.

"Alice?"

"Hello, Charlie."

"But . . . what . . . ?"

As I stood there openmouthed, Ma rose from her chair and took the rabbits from my hand. "Ya never told me ya 'ad a new friend, Charlie." She smiled. "And such a pretty one at that. How about I make us all a cup a tea?"

Not surprisingly, I was lost for words.

What was Alice Cornwall doing in my house?

Alice Cornwall hated my guts.

As she stepped toward me, I took a step back.

"I know what ya did, Charlie," she said softly, "and I wanted ta thank ya in person."

"But how did ya . . . ?"

"It wasn't hard. I asked around. Ya'd be surprised how many people know ya in Richmond."

Blushing, she lifted the lid on the cardboard box in her hands and pushed it under my nose.

"I know it's not much," she said, "but me and me dad wanted ya ta 'ave these."

Inside the box were four of the biggest cream buns I'd ever seen.

This time I knew exactly what to say.

"'Struth, they're monsters. What d'ya call 'em?"

Alice Cornwall threw me a smile, and I melted.

"We call 'em cream buns, genius."

At that moment, Ma returned to the living room with the tea. From the look on her face, I could tell she was enjoying the company.

"What say we 'ave another listen ta that record, eh, Alice?"

"That'd be nice, Mrs. Feehan. 'Ere, sit yerself down and I'll put it on fer ya."

Quite clearly, Ma was beside herself.

"Did ya 'appen to know, Charlie," she said, pouring the tea, "that me and Alice 'ave somethin' in common?"

"Is that right, Ma. And what would that be?"

"It just so 'appens that Alice loves ta dance."

Right then, the strangest thing happened. A vision of my father appeared in the living room as clear as Ma was sitting in the chair opposite. Standing near the fireplace he was, with one arm resting on the mantel. He raised his eyebrows, then smiled.

"Giddyup, Charlie." He winked.

Then he was gone.

If I'd had any doubts as to whether my ma had been cured of her condition, then I needn't have feared. She was unstoppable. While she and Alice took it in turns to replay the record, she was barely able to keep her trap shut.

Eleven times they played the record.

I'm forever blowing bubbles,

Pretty bubbles in the air. . . .

The way they talked, I had Buckley's of getting a word in, so instead I set about trying to solve one of life's more serious dilemmas.

How on earth was I going to fit a cream bun the size of a house brick into my mouth without making a mess?

Somehow I managed.

During the eleventh encore, I sensed that Alice was beginning to tire of the continuous stream of tiny bubbles being blown around our living room. So, during a rare lapse in the conversation, I called an end to the afternoon's festivities and somehow managed to steer Alice toward the front door. Once there, she thanked my ma and promised a return visit as soon as she could.

On the verandah I donned my cap, then pointed to the gate.

"Would ya let me walk ya home, Alice?" I asked.

"It's a bit outta ya way, ain't it, Charlie?" she replied.

"As a matter a fact, I'm 'eadin' that way meself. I've gotta pay someone a visit."

Suddenly there were daggers in her eyes.

"Don't worry, Alice. It ain't that kind a visit. Anyway, I could do with a walk after that cream bun. I'm in trainin', did ya know?"

"Trainin'? Fer what?"

"Runnin'. I'm entered in a mile race at Ballarat in a couple a weeks."

Not long into our walk, my words began to come easily. In a way, Alice reminded me of Nostrils. Like him, she never pushed things. She had a way of listening as if the very thing you were saying was feeding her, nourishing her in some way. And when she spoke, it was so infectious, I found myself wanting to tell her stuff in return—important stuff, stuff that meant a thing or two.

At the corner of Victoria Parade and Brunswick Street, the two of us stopped to say goodbye.

"Ya know, Ma'll come lookin' fer ya if ya don't come and visit 'er again," I said.

"I'm sure she will, Charlie. But don't worry, I'll be by again. Only, can ya do me a favor?"

"A course, Alice. Anythin'."

"Could ya per'aps think about addin' somethin' new ta yer record collection?"

"Good idea, Alice. I'll see what I can do."

As she went to leave, she turned as if she'd suddenly remembered something.

"I 'ope yer mate's awright, Charlie. It's a cryin' shame. . . . He sure could play."

Once again, white walls and hospital smells greeted me as I stepped into the casualty ward at St. Vincent's Hospital. There was a nurse stationed at the front desk.

"I'm 'ere ta see Norman Heath," I said.

Behind the counter, the nurse ran her finger down a list of names until she found *H*.

"Hanniberry . . . Haynes . . . Heaney . . ."

Finally her finger stopped.

"Here we go . . . Heath, Norman. Ward Six, third floor."

As I made my way toward another desk on the third floor, the events from the previous night came flooding back. I remembered the pink bubbles around Nostrils' mouth, his strangled groan as we crossed the tram tracks on Victoria Parade. And I remembered me, his mate, scratch-free.

Seeing me approach, the duty nurse rose to attention, then moved out from behind the desk until she was blocking my path.

Her white dress and cap indicated that she was someone trained in tending the sick, but the way she stood there, arms folded, she could well have passed for a Goodwood Street heavy.

I approached with caution.

"I'm here ta see Norman Heath, Sister," I said politely.

"He's just 'ad visitors. Unless you're family, you won't be going any further, I'm afraid."

"Me name's Charlie Heath, Sister. I'm 'is brother."

She studied me up close, searching for clues.

"His brother, eh?"

"That's right," I lied. "I'm the lucky one—didn't get the nose, thank God."

"Hmmm . . . All right, then, you can go through. Bed nine, 'e's in. You've only five minutes, though. And don't think I won't be counting."

"Thank you, Sister."

. . .

Strolling through the center of the room in my brown coat and pants, I suddenly felt out of place. Apart from the heads resting on the pillows, everything in Ward Six was white: the beds, the walls, and the floors.

At a guess, there were perhaps ten beds lined up on either side of me, each of them exactly the same distance apart. Even the white clipboards, hanging over the metal frames at the end of each bed, were perfectly aligned—courtesy, I daresay, of the sister in charge.

I found the silence in Ward Six unsettling.

It wasn't that I wished anyone ill health, but in a room full of sick people I'd expected one of them at least would be screaming or crying with pain. Instead, all twenty patients lay quietly in their beds like ghosts.

As a visitor, presumably in good health, I suddenly felt the urge to cough.

Bed nine was located toward the end of the row on my left.

While Nostrils lay there sleeping, I crept slowly forward and set about surveying the damage.

His left leg was slightly raised, resting on something hidden beneath the blankets. From the thigh down to the calf, a plaster cast, open at the top, acted like a cradle underneath his leg, for the purpose of keeping it straight. Spots of blood were visible on the wad of bandages around his knee.

Farther up, there were bandages around his ribs, too. Somewhere underneath the blankets, a plastic tube pierced his side. I followed its length and saw that it ran into a bottle hanging from the side of his bed.

In the bottle was an inch or so of pink foam.

Gently, I reached out and touched Nostrils' arm.

"Nostrils," I said softly. "It's Charlie."

Opening his eyes, even a little way, seemed a struggle. When he saw it was me, he shifted a little higher on the pillow and grabbed at his ribs in pain.

"Charlie," he whispered. "Ya took yer time comin' ta visit, didn't ya?"

"Yeah, sorry. Thought I'd let ya settle in first. How are ya, Nostrils?"

"I've been better, I'll give ya the nod. Hand me that glass a water, will ya? I'm as dry as a hotel gone six o'clock."

Even in distress, Nostrils found a reason to joke. Suddenly I could no longer hide my shame.

"I'm sorry, Nostrils," I said, handing him the water. "I'm real sorry."

"What are ya sorry about, Charlie?"

"I'm sorry I left ya like that. It's some mate I turned out ta be. I should a listened ta ya. You was right, Nostrils. So was me mum. It's all gettin' too dangerous. As soon as ya get outta 'ere, I'm gunna join ya at Rosella's. I'm gunna do somethin' respectable."

"Don't go blamin' yerself, Charlie. It's me own fault fer slippin' over. There ain't no point the two of us bein' laid up in 'ere. . . . Anyway, I don't reckon I could stand ya lyin' beside me all day. Ya'd drive me nuts, ya would."

"I never should a left ya, Nostrils."

"Flamin' 'eck, would ya stop blabbin'? Ya supposed ta be cheerin' me up, ain't ya? Come on, what 'ave ya been doin' these last few days?"

A tear rolled down my face as I looked at his busted knee.

What could I possibly say?

It was Nostrils who was the champion. He was something special, a freak. It should have been me lying there, not him.

"Come on, Charlie," he said again. "What 'ave ya been doin'? How's the trainin'?"

With the sleeve of my coat I wiped away the tears.

"Everythin's on track."

"That's beaut. Ya must be flyin' by now. Ya'll murder 'em, Charlie."

Suddenly Nostrils was all smiles.

"He 'asn't got yer on the two F's again, 'as 'e?"

"A course. There ain't nothin' surer. He's got me rabbitin', too."

"Rabbitin'?"

"Yeah, down at Yarra Park. Ain't caught one yet, but I'm gettin' close."

Far too soon, the sister appeared and pointed to her watch.

"Ya'd better go, Charlie. She's a right boiler, that one."

"Awright, Nostrils. Are ya up fer a visit tomorra?"

"Too right I am. I'm bored outta me brain in 'ere. I'll see ya soon, Charlie. And stop blamin' yerself. It weren't yer fault."

A dose of Norman Heath—there was no better medicine for raising one's spirits.

Where it came from I do not know, but as I strode back toward Richmond, I felt the need for a song.

I'm forever blowin' bubbles,

Pretty bubbles in the air. . . .

Admittedly, I hadn't much of an ear for music, but as I arrived at Squizzy's place after the eighth rendition, parts of the song were sounding surprisingly tuneful.

A few seconds after I knocked on the door, the metal plate slid open once again.

"Yeah?"

"Knuckles, it's me, Charlie."

As he opened the door, Knuckles flashed me a smile.

"How are ya this fine evenin', Charlie?"

"Fightin' fit, Knuckles. What about yerself?"

"Couldn't be better, lad."

Before he made to leave, I grabbed at his sleeve and stopped him.

"Can ya tell me where Dolly is, Knuckles?" I asked. "She ain't been around of late."

Knuckles glanced over his shoulder down the hall, then leaned my way.

"Er . . . Squiz and Doll . . . they . . . er . . ."

"They what?"

"They had a tiff, Charlie. She packed her bags and cleared out."

"He kicked her out, didn't he?"

"It ain't my business, lad, and it ain't yers, either. Stop pokin' yer nose where it don't belong."

That was the end of it. Shattered, I followed Knuckles down the hall to the office and stepped in after him.

Half a dozen men were gathered in the office, Dasher and Squizzy among them. They were drinking a toast.

"And 'ere's ta the Richmond push," roared Squizzy,

holding his whisky aloft. "Yas all did us proud last night, lads."

As one, the others raised their glasses in response.

"Cheers!" came the reply.

After the toast, Squizzy spotted me at the door.

"'Ere's me speedster now. Come in, lad, we're celebratin'. D'ya fancy a spot a whisky?"

"No, thanks, Mr. Taylor."

"Knuckles! Get the lad a spot a whisky."

By the look of him, Squizzy had been drinking awhile. He drained the last of his glass, then slammed it down onto the desk.

"Come on, Knuckles," he slurred. "A man ain't a camel, ya know."

While he waited for a refill, Squizzy drew my attention to the newspapers scattered across the desk.

"Ain't no one gunna mess with Squizzy Taylor, lad. 'Ave ya copped the papers yet?"

"No, Mr. Taylor, I ain't."

As Knuckles handed me a glass, I stepped forward and read the headline: "Guns Bark in Fitzroy!"

"And what about this one?" said Squizzy, holding a paper aloft. "'Popgunitis!' That's me favorite. I'll 'ave ta get me photograph with that one."

Standing there, in the room full of men, I began to feel uncomfortable.

"Mr. Taylor," I said, "if ya don't mind, I wanna talk ta ya about the liquor run last night."

Annoyed by my lack of interest in the headlines, Squizzy threw the paper onto the desk, then considered me with as much excitement as you'd have for a blowfly with a belly full of maggots.

"I'm glad ya reminded me, lad. I clear forgot with all the excitement from the shootin'. A fella from Goodwood Street called . . . somethin' about a trolley?"

"We got rolled in the gardens comin' back from the job, Mr. Taylor. I used it ta take me mate Norman ta the 'ospital. He's busted up real bad."

I hated having to explain myself in front of the others. Suddenly, as quick as someone flicking a switch, Squizzy turned nasty.

"To tell ya the truth, lad, I couldn't give a rat's arse about yer mate. Get that trolley back where it belongs. Now clear off. We're celebratin' 'ere, and yer beginnin' ta get on me nerves."

Even though my back was to them, I could hear the men behind me laughing. Full of rage, I dropped my eyes to the ground and saw my shiny black boots. Right then, something clicked inside my head. Everything became clear. Silently I left the office and made my way to the laundry. After changing into my father's old boots, I strode back down the hall. I squeezed past Knuckles at the office door and placed the boots on the table, right under Squizzy's nose.

"And what the bloody 'ell is this?" he asked.

"It's yer boots, Mr. Taylor. . . . Ya know, it's funny, but they never really fit me in the first place."

Squizzy exploded. From a desk drawer he produced a silver handgun and pointed it between my eyes.

"Squiz!"

Suddenly Dasher Heeney was standing beside me.

"C'mon, Squiz, he's only a lad."

Despite the wildness in Squizzy's eyes, I felt remarkably calm.

Without moving an inch, I waited for the flip of the coin.

Heads or tails.

Yes or no.

Go or stay.

In a split second, Squizzy shifted the silver barrel to the left of my head and fired a shot into the wall.

When I opened my eyes, only two people remained standing.

Me and Squizzy Taylor.

"I'll give yer one thing, lad," he said. "Fer a young'un, yer've got a set a balls on ya. Now get out before me aim improves."

With my heart racing, I followed Knuckles down the hall, then stopped. Looking back, I saw Squizzy's head poking out the door, an idiotic grin plastered across his face.

"What was ya expectin', ya little runt? Did ya want me ta send yer mate a bunch a flowers or somethin'?"

Out in the street, there was nothing to do but run.

With a ringing in my ears, I headed west at such a speed that the streets of Richmond rolled into one. It seemed like forever since I'd run like this, without a purpose—without a list of names or a parcel to deliver.

As I hurtled up Punt Road, I felt the city lights beckoning once again. I felt the prickle of my skin and the sweat on my brow.

When I made it to the city, I began whooping and hollering like a mad thing. I dodged drunks and played with cars, I jumped over puddles and raced alongside grinding trams.

For the first time in a long while, I felt free again, as if a huge weight had been lifted from my shoulders.

My days running for Squizzy Taylor were over.

Now I was running for me.

CHAPTER NINETEEN

By the end of my second week's training, the rabbits at Yarra Park had an extra reason to be scared. I was flying. Besides the rabbiting, twice a week Mr. Redmond and I caught the tram to St. Kilda Beach. While the children played games near the water's edge, Mr. Redmond had me running barefoot in the soft sand beside the foreshore. Stripped to my knickerbockers and singlet, I must have looked a sight to those who stopped to watch.

Two trees on the foreshore, some ninety yards apart, acted as markers. My instructions were simple enough—sprint up, turn, then jog back.

I was useless at first. After my first few sprints, a small crowd had gathered beside Mr. Redmond as I struggled in the sand. Some of them, I noticed, were laughing.

"C'mon, Charlie," barked Mr. Redmond. "Sprint!"

Soon the others were joining in.

"C'mon, lad, ya'll be goin' backwards before long."

I didn't mind the jeering.

In fact, if anything, it made me more determined. So did the burning pain in my legs—instead of fighting it, I welcomed it and used it to make myself strong.

While Clarrie busied himself chasing seagulls, I continued running.

Sprint, jog, sprint, jog.

"Fink about what yer doin', Charlie," called Mr. Redmond. "Ya ain't runnin' the streets now, lad."

Jogging back to the first marker, I noticed a row of children in front of Mr. Redmond, sitting on the bluestone wall, watching me. A pretty girl at the end of the line cupped her hand around her mouth and shouted.

"C'mon, Charlie. You can do it."

Sensing a game was about to begin, the others began kicking their heels playfully against the wall.

"Yeah, c'mon, Charlie!"

Smiling, I turned at the marker and dropped my eyes.

Go!

Spurred on by the children, I began to shorten my stride. I dug my toes deep into the shifting sand and pushed.

"Attaboy, Charlie," called Mr. Redmond. "Now yer finkin'."

For ten minutes I continued running, each time getting faster and faster.

Then, one by one, the children jumped from the wall, barefoot, and joined me on the beach. With my training nearly done, I slowed my pace until there were a dozen of them chasing behind me, digging their toes into the sand.

In the weeks leading up to race day, all hell broke loose.

The rival gangs in Richmond and Fitzroy went head to head in a bloody battle so violent that the sound of gunfire was a regular occurrence in the streets at night. Each day, it seemed, the front pages of the newspapers reported a fresh wave of shootings, adding names to the growing list of those wounded or killed.

They called it the Fitzroy Vendetta.

Gangsterism had arrived.

While those around me drew their curtains and locked their doors, I continued my nightly runs through the city streets. Running was everything now, and I would stop for no one. I was invincible.

Still, while my body grew strong, something kept nagging away in my head.

Then one night as I returned home from my run, I suddenly realized what it was that was troubling me. It was Ma.

I found her in the living room listening to one of the new records I'd bought. Seeing me, she smiled and craned her head toward the gramophone in the corner.

"Ya know, 'andsome, if ya play yer cards right, ya can write yer name on me dance card if ya like."

Without speaking, I went to the gramophone and lifted the needle from the record.

"Charlie, what is it?"

"I need ta talk ta ya, Ma."

"A course. What's up?"

I sat in the chair next to her, then shifted forward.

"I gotta tell ya somethin', Ma, and I don't think ya gunna like it. . . . I ain't goin' ta school no more. I've been workin' fer Squizzy Taylor."

Next to me, Ma dropped her eyes and began studying her shoes.

"Ma . . . did ya not hear me? I said I been workin' fer Squizzy Taylor."

"I know what yer been doin', Charlie. I ain't daft."

"Ya do? But . . ."

"I know a lot a things, Charlie."

She turned her face to the fire and ran a finger across the scar above her left eye.

"Things 'ave changed," she said softly. "We're on our own now, Charlie. Ain't nothin' gunna bring yer father back."

"Yer right, Ma. But at least we got each other. First thing after the race, I'm gunna get me a job at Rosella's. Somethin' respectable, like ya said. Ya'll see . . . things'll be different from now on, Ma, I promise."

For a few minutes the two of us sat quietly, staring into the fire. Finally it was Ma who broke the silence.

"Mrs. Redmond tells me yer trainin' hard for the race."

"That's right, Ma. Mr. Redmond's got me rabbitin', and runnin' on the beach."

"Rabbitin', hey? 'Ave ya got any yet?"

"Not yet, Ma, but I'm givin' Clarrie a run fer 'is money, I can tell ya. Still, it's a different thing, runnin' a race."

"Ya'll be right, Charlie. If I was a bettin' lady, I'd put me money on yer."

"Ya would?"

"Course. . . . Now, how about that dance?"

On the Thursday before we left for Ballarat, I met Alice outside St. Vincent's Hospital as arranged. When I arrived, she was already standing out front, a splash of red on an otherwise gray and dreary canvas. She looked even more beautiful than I'd remembered. Her hair was gathered at the back, held in place by a tortoiseshell comb. In her hands she carried an umbrella and a cardboard box.

She smiled. "It's a day fer ducks, I reckon, Charlie."

"Yer right there, Alice. How are ya?"

"All the better fer seein' you, Charlie."

Like no one else, Alice Cornwall had a way of making my heart race. Suddenly even the simple task of walking seemed a struggle.

"Are ya awright, Charlie?" she asked as we made our way toward the hospital doors.

"Ta tell ya the truth, Alice, I'm feelin' a little faint. I've a good mind ta check meself in ta see a doctor."

Soon we arrived on the third floor, Ward Six. With my mind turned to mush, I'd completely forgotten to warn Alice about Knuckles' twin sister manning the desk.

"Family only," she announced, stepping into the corridor.

"Charlie Heath, Sister," I said. "I'm here ta see Norman."

As she folded her arms, her eyes shifted to Alice.

"And you are?"

Next to me, my beautiful companion transformed herself into Saint Alice.

"Alice Cornwall, Sister. I'm Norman's cousin. I would 'ave come earlier, but I've been flat-out carin' fer me dyin' nan."

Even though I knew her words to be a giant fib, I raised my arm up and placed it gently across her shoulder.

"God bless you, Alice," said the sister. "Have you ever thought about nursing as a profession? It's girls like you we need."

"I 'ave, Sister. It's somethin' I always wanted ta do."

"In that case, you can go on through. And take your time, won't you."

As we made our way along Ward Six, Alice flashed me a cheeky smile.

"Flamin' 'eck, Alice," I said. "Ferget about the nursin'. With a heart a gold like yers, ya'd be better off tryin' fer the convent."

At bed nine we found Nostrils awake.

"Hello there," he chirped. "I see ya brought a visitor with ya, Charlie."

"Norman Heath, I'd like ya ta meet Alice Cornwall."

Nostrils smiled.

"Ya 'ave been busy, Charlie. Hello, Alice, it's nice ta meet ya."

"You too, Norman," replied Alice. "'Ere, I've brought somethin' fer ya."

Carefully, she placed the cardboard box on his stomach, then opened the lid.

"'Struth, they're monsters. What d'ya call 'em?"

Alice and I looked at each other and laughed.

"Ya must be jokin', Nostrils," I said. "Ain't ya never seen a cream bun before?"

Just as I'd known they would, Alice and Nostrils took an instant shine to each other. For a good half hour the three of us sat talking as if we'd known each other for years. We could have talked for hours, but soon Nostrils began to tire.

"If you two insist on makin' me laugh," he said, grabbing his ribs, "I'll 'ave ta kick ya out. How am I supposed ta get better if yas keep muckin' around? Go on, clear off, ya ratbags."

As I rose from my chair, Nostrils grabbed hold of my arm and looked at me with heavy eyes.

"Ya'll be right in the race. Yer a freak, Charlie Feehan. Ain't no one faster than you. Ya'll murder 'em. They may as well start engravin' yer name on the cup."

With his hand still on my arm, Nostrils closed his eyes and drifted off to sleep.

Outside the hospital, as we sheltered from the rain, Alice Cornwall slipped her arm into mine. Then slowly, she raised herself on tiptoe and kissed my cheek.

"Here," she said, slipping an envelope into my coat pocket. "I want ya ta read it when ya get ta Ballarat."

"I'll be runnin' fer ya, Alice," I said.

"No, Charlie," she replied. "Don't run fer me. Run fer yerself."

Mindful of Mr. Redmond's advice not to overdo it before the big race, I fought the urge to run, and instead walked at an easy pace toward home. My preparation for the race could not have been better—the muscles in my legs were testament to that. Still, each time I filled my head with a positive thought, some frightening doubt grabbed hold of it and hit it clear for six. Over and over I imagined the race at Ballarat—the start, the bends, and the finish—until eventually I found myself outside Porter's Wood Yard in Church Street.

Imagine owning a wood yard. . . .

As I stood there staring at the FOR SALE sign, a familiar voice sounded in my head. It was Daisy, the prostitute who lived on our street. As I remembered her words, everything became clear.

Whatever ya do, Charlie, she'd said, *use the money fer somethin' good . . . somethin' good . . . somethin' good. . . .*

The next morning, when I woke, there was nothing on my wall—no dogs, no dragons, and no faces. Just mold.

With my bag already packed, I dressed in a clean set of clothes, then slid the box of newspapers out from under the bed. I hadn't counted my savings for a while, and the envelope felt surprisingly fat. I opened it and emptied the contents onto the floor. In the time I'd been working for Squizzy Taylor, my earnings, plus tips, totaled twenty-three quid and five bob.

It was a fortune.

As I sat against the bed, the stash reminded me of the play money my father used to make me, and how I'd pile it into neat rows, always asking for more.

What are ya gunna buy, Charlie? he'd ask.

I'm gunna buy a horse, Daddy, I'd say. *A horse and a big silver cart.*

And what else, Charlie? Yer've still got more.

Some beer fer you and a dress fer Ma.

Twenty-three pounds and five shillings!

It was enough to buy a dozen dresses and more. But this was no longer a game, and I was no longer a boy.

Anyway, my mind was already made up. Quickly I gathered together the money, placed it back in the envelope, and stuffed it safely into my trouser pocket.

After a breakfast of bread and jam, Ma, Jack, and I met the Redmonds on our front porch.

"C'mon, Charlie," said Mr. Redmond. "We best get goin' if we're ta make the train."

When I turned to Ma, she was crying.

"I'll be right, Ma," I said. "It's only fer a night."

"I know, I know."

With Jack between us, she drew me in and squeezed me tight.

"Yer father'd be so proud of yer, Charlie."

Over her shoulder I could see Mr. Redmond planting kisses on Clarrie's snout.

Mrs. Redmond looked annoyed.

"Flamin' 'eck, Cecil," she protested. "Anyone'd think ya were married ta 'im, the way yer carryin' on. What about me?"

"Don't ya worry, luv, I got plenty ta go 'round."

With the goodbyes complete, Mr. Redmond and I gathered our bags and headed toward Spencer Street Station. Two doors down he stopped and doubled back to our front gate. The others were still where we'd left them.

"Remember ta put 'is coat on 'im if it gets too cold, luv," he called to his wife. "It's the tartan one he likes. Don't go puttin' that silly blue one on 'im, it'll make 'im scratch."

CHAPTER TWENTY

Arriving at Spencer Street reminded me of the times my father and I would come and watch the trains. I remember being fascinated, even from an early age, by the steam trains and the way they roared to life, shooting plumes of black smoke from their chimneys like gigantic beasts.

They'd terrified me at first. Holding on to my father's trousers, I'd poke my head out from between his legs and watch in horror as people climbed aboard, then disappeared into the bowels of the hissing monster.

It had been the stuff of nightmares. Under my blankets at night, I'd often found myself back on the platform, running along the line of people waiting to board. I'd be shouting at them, pleading with them not to go, but they could not hear. Instead, the monster drew them in and they went happily, old and young, to what I imagined was a grisly and gruesome death.

Now, a little braver and somewhat wiser, I stood in that same line on the platform, wild with excitement. I couldn't wait to climb aboard and begin the journey to Ballarat. Except for a weekend at the seaside in Sandringham, I'd never really ventured far from home.

As the railway porters lugged the bags of the well-to-do up

to the first-class carriages, the stationmaster, in his dark green uniform and cap, walked in front of us ringing his bell.

"All aboard to Ballarat. . . . All aboard!"

Even though Ballarat was only a few hours by train, I was so excited, it was as if the two of us were about to set sail for one of those distant places I'd read about in my school history book—a place far away, where the people wore feathered head-dresses and carried spears.

Next to me, Mr. Redmond turned and smiled.

"This is it, Charlie," he said. "Are ya ready?"

"Are ya kiddin', Mr. Redmond? C'mon, if ya don't hurry up we'll miss a window seat."

With Mr. Redmond close behind, I boarded the train and slipped into a seat beside the window. Inside, the train smelt like varnish. The seats were slippery leather, and the metal luggage racks above our heads shone a brilliant gold.

Not far to my right, a well-dressed young man removed his hat, placed a bag on the seat opposite me, and clicked it open. With his back to me, he took something from it, then tossed the bag up onto the rack. When he sat down, my eyes were instantly drawn to his lap. There in front of me was one of the most beautiful sights I'd ever seen—a pair of spotless white running spikes.

"Yer entered in the Mile, are ya?" I asked.

He looked up briefly, then returned to inspecting the shoes.

"That's right."

"Me too. Mr. Redmond 'ere's me trainer. 'Ave ya got a trainer yerself?"

"I'm with the Melbourne Harriers. Have been for three years."

"It's a runnin' club, is it?"

"That's right. I should be up in first class with the others, only some idiot mixed up my ticket."

"I don't s'pose ya been doin' any rabbitin', then?"

"Excuse me?"

"Rabbitin'. Mr. Redmond 'ere's 'ad me rabbitin' down at Yarra Park. Been runnin' in the sand as well. Ya know, fer speed."

"Speed?" he laughed. "It's a mile race, not a sprint. Anyone who knows a thing or two about running knows that it's distance you need in a mile—distance, not speed. And good Lord, no . . . I certainly haven't been rabbiting."

As the young man went back to inspecting his spikes, I turned to Mr. Redmond, who was busy reading the program.

"Psst!" I whispered. "When ya say ya did a bit a runnin', Mr. Redmond . . . what exactly did ya mean?"

Before raising his eyes, Mr. Redmond put a finger on the program to mark his spot.

"Huh?"

"When ya say ya did a bit a runnin'," I repeated, "what exactly did ya mean?"

Mr. Redmond looked beyond the window as if he was remembering a time long ago.

"It were a bloke by the name a Piggy Devlin who got me runnin'," he said.

"He were yer trainer, were 'e?"

"Nah, 'e were the school bully. Used ta chase me 'ome from school."

"Hang on a jiff. I thought ya said ya ran serious."

"It *were* serious, Charlie. He would a killed me 'ad 'e caught

me." As a whistle sounded outside, I turned away from Mr. Redmond and poked my head out the window for a look. While a small crowd of people waved goodbye to their loved ones, the stationmaster produced a white flag and began waving it in the air. Then, as if the train had a mind of its own, it tooted loudly and lurched itself forward. We were away.

When I pulled my head inside, no one seemed the slightest bit interested in our departure except for a couple of children a few rows away. Next to me, Mr. Redmond lifted his right leg over his left and leaned my way.

"It says 'ere that yer ta run a heat in the mornin'," he whispered. "There's five heats all up, and the first three place-getters from each one move inta the final in the afternoon. Let's see . . . that makes it a field a fifteen—well, fourteen plus yerself."

On the seat opposite, the young man began to snigger.

"Somethin' funny?" asked Mr. Redmond.

"Yeah. I was just wondering how it is you get the rabbit to run around the track without nicking off?"

"Ignore 'im, Charlie."

"I've seen some of those rabbits up in Ballarat, you know, and I can tell you, they're not as smart as your city bunnies. Maybe you should have brought one up with you. A specialist miler, perhaps."

Mr. Redmond was all set to go on with it when a man in a green uniform pushed through the carriage door.

"Tickets, please! Tickets!"

While the others searched for their tickets, I turned my head and gazed out the window. At a guess we'd been traveling for a good half hour, with the city now well behind us. Except

for the occasional shack, there was nothing to see except cows and sheep and paddocks. It was a far cry from the streets of Richmond, where the houses were packed so tight it felt as if the air was being squeezed from your lungs. But I couldn't imagine running in a place with nothing to see—a place without lights and trams, grog joints and brothels.

True, I lived in a city that was home to every imaginable evil, but for me, there was always something else.

For me there was always hope.

Sometime later the landscape began to change. Through the window I spotted a couple of the digs I'd read about in school. Not so long ago, thousands of people had flocked to Ballarat to dig up the earth in search of gold. Of those thousands, only a few had been lucky enough to strike it rich.

The massive holes with the dirt piled up next to them looked like the work of some giant rabbit. I could not believe that someone had dug into the land like that, bored into it, day after day.

I tried to picture the men who'd dug the holes—men with blistered hands and broken backs. What had driven them to such lengths?

Looking out across the fields, I suddenly realized what it was. These men were just like me. These men had dreamed of something more, something better.

Even just a slice.

Soon enough, other things began to creep into the landscape outside: a bluestone fence, compliments of a convict gang; a man on a horse and cart; livestock; houses and church spires. Finally, we had arrived in Ballarat.

As the train screeched its way to a halt, the young man opposite rose to his feet and retrieved his bag.

"I suppose I should be thankful in a way," he said.

Mr. Redmond stiffened.

"And why is that, son?"

"You're one less runner I'll have to worry about. See you at the track."

By the time we stepped onto the crowded platform, the young man's comments seemed like a distant memory. My eyes began searching the faces of the people around me. I sharpened my ears for new sounds and sniffed at strange smells. As we pushed through the crowd, I suddenly remembered the wad of money in my trouser pocket. Quickly I shot my hand down and gripped the envelope tight.

Out in the street, Mr. Redmond took a map from his bag and straightened it.

"Awright, then, Charlie," he said. "We're lookin' fer a Mrs. Pickwick's lodgin' 'ouse in George Street. It's this way, I think. C'mon, follow me and we'll get ourselves settled in."

After a short walk, we arrived at the lodging house in George Street and were greeted by a jolly lady in a floral dress. She had eyes like an owl—big and brown and wide.

"Evenin'," she said as she opened the door. "Ya must be Mr. Redmond."

"That I am, Mrs. Pickwick. And this 'ere is Charlie."

"Hello, Charlie. Welcome ta Ballarat. Everythin's ready fer ya. Come on in and we'll get ya settled."

At the end of the hallway, Mrs. Pickwick stood beside a bedroom door and ushered us in.

"There ya go." She smiled. "It ain't nothin' fancy, but ya'll find it's nice and clean. How about I leave ya to it? And if there's anythin' ya need, make sure ta sing out. I've a spot a dinner on the go. Should be ready fer ya, say, around six."

"Thank you, Mrs. Pickwick," said Mr. Redmond. "It's a lovely 'ome ya 'ave. Me and Charlie'll be fine."

From the way she smiled, I could tell that Mrs. Pickwick, like my ma, prided herself on a clean house. Our room was a decent size, with two beds on either side. On each of the beds, she'd left two white towels folded so neatly it seemed a shame to disturb them.

"Go on, then, Charlie," said Mr. Redmond. "Take yer pick."

I picked the bed near the window and dropped my bag on top of the mattress.

"If ya don't mind, Mr. Redmond," I joked, "I'll take the one with the view."

"Awright, Charlie. Get yer things sorted. There's somethin' I want ta show ya before it gets dark."

My things, as Mr. Redmond called them, consisted of a toothbrush, a clean pair of socks, a singlet, fresh underwear, and some short pants. I transferred them to the top drawer of the bedside table, then sat on the bed and waited. When I looked across the room, Mr. Redmond was sitting on his bed next to his open bag, smiling.

"There's just somethin' else before we get goin', Charlie. Come over 'ere. . . . A few a the neighbors chipped in ta buy ya somethin'. They ain't as flash as that fella's on the train, but I'm thinkin' they'll take a few seconds off yer time."

As I sat on the bed next to him, Mr. Redmond handed me a pair of black running spikes.

"They're leather ones, Charlie," he said. "Light as a feather."

Polished 'em meself, I did. Go on, 'ave a whiff. Ya can still smell the nugget."

Lost for words, I cradled the spikes in my hands so delicately, it was as if Mr. Redmond had just handed me a bird with a broken wing.

"I don't know what ta say, Mr. Redmond," I managed. "Me very own spikes."

"Ya can thank me later, Charlie. C'mon, put 'em away, we've gotta go."

Out in the front garden, Mrs. Pickwick was bent over the veggie patch, pulling up that night's dinner. When she saw us, she straightened up, then wiped her hands on her apron.

"Off already, are yas?" she asked.

"Just fer a bit," answered Mr. Redmond. "Never fear, Mrs. Pickwick, we'll be back fer dinner."

As we walked down George Street, while Mr. Redmond studied the map, I lifted my hands and smelt the nugget on my fingers. It made me think of Dolly and the way she had lifted her wrist to my nose after spraying it with one of Madame Ghurka's latest scents.

"Where are ya takin' us, Mr. Redmond?"

"Ya'll see, Charlie. It's only another block."

The streets of Ballarat told a different story from the one I was accustomed to. The air was crisp and clean, and the people, whenever they passed, smiled and said hello. In Ballarat there was room to move. The streets seemed wider, less crowded, giving me the impression that things were moving more slowly.

As we turned another corner, Mr. Redmond folded his map and tucked it into a pocket.

"'Ere we go, Charlie—Centennial Park."

West across the horizon, a dying sun took its last few stubborn breaths, then finally surrendered to the night. On the oval, a few runners were packing up their gear and heading home.

"C'mon, Charlie," said Mr. Redmond. "I want ya ta walk a lap with me."

I don't know why I did it, but as I followed Mr. Redmond out onto the running track, I shortened my stride to avoid stepping on the white lines that marked the lanes. Somehow it didn't seem right.

When he saw what I was up to, he laughed.

"It's awright, Charlie. We're not 'ere fer a game a hopscotch. Ya can step on the lines—no one's gunna kick ya off."

I ignored him and kept stepping between the lines until the two of us were standing in the inside lane. Lane one.

Mr. Redmond put a hand on my shoulder, then pointed to our feet.

"D'ya see where we're standin', Charlie?" he asked.

"It's lane number one, Mr. Redmond."

"That's right, lane one. C'mon, let's walk a lap."

As we strode across the soft grass, Mr. Redmond continued talking.

"Right 'ere, Charlie, this is where I want ya ta be. If ya 'ave ta go wide, yer ta do it in the straight. But whatever ya do, don't swing wide on the bends. Ya got that?"

"I understand, Mr. Redmond."

"Tell me what I said, so I know ya got it."

"If I 'ave ta go wide, do it in the straight, but stay on the inside lane on the bends."

"Good lad. . . . Now, there's likely ta be a bit a rough stuff durin' the race. The bigger blokes may knock yer 'round. But don't let 'em scare ya, Charlie. Just stay outta trouble as best ya can. And remember, don't swing wide on the bends."

Soon enough we were back where we started.

"Four a those, Charlie," said Mr. Redmond. "Four laps. Ya could do it in yer sleep."

CHAPTER TWENTY-ONE

When we arrived back at the lodging house just before six o'clock, Mrs. Pickwick had the table set ready for dinner.

"I'm hopin' the two a ya like rabbit stew," she said, bringing three plates to the table. "It's not somethin' ya'd be used ta, bein' from the city an' all."

Mr. Redmond flashed me a wink, then smiled.

"It's a real treat, Mrs. Pickwick. And the vegetables . . . I noticed ya grow yer own?"

"That I do, Mr. Redmond. The veggie patch was me late 'usband's pride and joy. He 'ad a thing fer growin' 'is own— 'specially tomatoes. Loved 'is tomatoes, 'e did."

"Well, I ain't seen a finer patch than the one yer keepin', Mrs. Pickwick. Yer've a green thumb on yer, that's fer sure."

I don't deny that having a green thumb is an admirable quality in a woman, and something to be proud of, but the way Mrs. Pickwick blushed, it was as if she'd just been complimented on the color of her eyes. She began patting her chest, as if her heart was aflutter, then raised her free hand up to a mop of gray hair and smoothed it flat.

"Mr. Redmond, yer too kind."

"Credit where it's due, Mrs. Pickwick. Credit where it's

due. . . . By the way, I read in yer advertisement that yer've an interest in the readin' of palms?"

"That I 'ave, Mr. Redmond. I've been studyin' the art a fortune-tellin' in me spare time. I'm only an amateur, mind you, but I've already a list a clients that see me regular."

Suddenly I remembered the wad of money in my pocket.

"D'ya think ya could read me palm, Mrs. Pickwick?" I asked excitedly, shooting my left hand across the table.

It was the first time I'd spoken since we'd sat down for dinner.

"I don't know, Charlie," she said. "Are ya sure it's a good idea? Yer've the big race tomorrow."

"C'mon," I said. "It's a bit a fun, is all."

Beside me, Mr. Redmond shrugged.

"Don't s'pose it'd hurt," he said. "That's if yer willin', a course, Mrs. Pickwick."

Mrs. Pickwick placed her knife and fork on her plate, then straightened herself in her chair.

"Awright, then, but I'll need yer right 'and, Charlie."

I too dropped my knife onto my plate, and I offered her my hand.

She took it, then studied my palm while she sucked at a scrap of food that had lodged itself between her teeth. After only a few minutes she lifted her head and looked at me with her wide brown eyes.

"I'm sorry fer yer loss, Charlie," she said softly. "I see yer've 'ad a rough trot these past few months."

If it wasn't for the tabletop, I reckon my jaw would have dropped all the way to the floor.

"But, Mrs. Pickwick . . . how did ya . . . ?"

"It's in yer 'and, Charlie. Once ya know what ta look fer, it's no different ta readin' a book."

"'Struth. . . . And what about the race, Mrs. Pickwick?"

"Hmmm, let's see."

This time Mrs. Pickwick put her hand in mine and closed her eyes.

"Hmmm."

"What is it? D'ya see somethin'?"

Before answering, she squeezed my hand a little harder.

"I see somethin' awright, Charlie, but there's no faces."

"There's not? What is there, then?"

"Runnin' shoes."

"Runnin' shoes?"

"Yeah, runnin' shoes. A pair a white and a pair a black . . . Hang on a jiff, there's more."

"What is it?" I asked.

Before she was able to give me more, Mrs. Pickwick shook her head, then released her grip.

"Nah, it's gone," she replied, opening her eyes. "I'm sorry, Charlie. That's it, I'm afraid."

"What d'ya mean, that's it?"

"I've lost it, Charlie. It can 'appen sometimes."

"Can't ya try again?"

"I'm afraid not, Charlie. They've told me everythin' they want ya ta hear."

"They?"

"The spirit world, Charlie. It ain't polite ta be askin' fer more. That's it."

"But—"

"Charlie!"

Beside me, Mr. Redmond put his hand on my arm.

"There ain't no more, Charlie," he said. "C'mon, eat yer dinner."

As I picked at a rabbit bone, I tried to make sense of what I'd just been told. Mrs. Pickwick hadn't told me anything I didn't already know. In a footrace of this kind, there were bound to be running shoes, some black and some white. So, just who those shoes belonged to was anyone's guess.

After dinner, Mr. Redmond and I excused ourselves, then headed off to our room for an early night. Stripped to my singlet and underwear, I placed my new running shoes under the blankets, then dived in beside them.

"Get yerself a good night's sleep, Charlie," said Mr. Redmond from the other side of the room. "Just remember all the work ya done. Yer've made me real proud these last few weeks, as if ya were me own son. Yer father'd be mighty proud, too, I know 'e would. Good night, Charlie. I'll see ya in the mornin'."

With the smell of nugget in my nose, I began to think of the hours I'd spent running. It wasn't just the hours at Yarra Park or St. Kilda Beach I thought of. I went back to that first time I'd ventured out—that time I'd plotted a course of four main streets to rid myself of the cold, dull ache in my bones. Tomorrow, however, I'd be running for something more. I'd be running for my father, for Ma, for Jack, for Alice, for Nostrils, and for Mr. Redmond. Tomorrow I'd be running the race of my life, and the stakes were high.

Clutching my running shoes to my chest, I turned my face to the other side of the room.

"Good night, Mr. Redmond," I whispered.

"Good night, Charlie."

Next morning, I woke to the smell of nugget. Mr. Redmond was already up, so I leapt from the bed, dressed, then joined him in the kitchen. Mrs. Pickwick was sitting at the table opposite him.

"'Ere 'e is now, Mr. Redmond," she said. "Did ya sleep awright, Charlie?"

"Like a log, Mrs. Pickwick."

"And 'ow are ya feelin'?" asked Mr. Redmond.

"I'm feelin' fast, as it 'appens."

"Good lad. Sit yerself down and 'ave some toast. And get some water into ya. I don't want ya thirsty before the race. We've only an 'our and a 'alf before yer heat."

After a light breakfast, Mr. Redmond and I packed our gear and said goodbye to Mrs. Pickwick at the front door. As I went to step off the porch, she cupped my face in her hands and kissed me on the cheek.

"I just thought ya'd like ta know, Charlie," she said. "It's never 'appened ta me before, but last night, I 'ad a vision in me sleep. Those black runnin' shoes I was tellin' ya about—they was yers, Charlie."

"Really?"

"As clear as day . . . Good luck, Charlie. I'll be along ta see ya later."

With a spring in my step, I walked alongside Mr. Redmond to the track.

"Don't go gettin' carried away, now," he said.

"But, Mr. Redmond, she 'ad a vision. And she knew about me father, too."

"Just concentrate on the runnin', Charlie. That's what we're 'ere fer."

Soon enough we arrived at Centennial Park. Already, a large group of runners was gathered on the oval in the center of the track, warming up. Since last night, two white marquees had been erected on the grass directly in front of the small grandstand. From my experience running for Squizzy Taylor, I knew one of them to be the bookmakers' tent. The other, just as crowded, seemed to be serving refreshments.

"I wonder what odds they've got me at," I said casually.

"They won't 'ave 'em posted till the final, Charlie," replied Mr. Redmond. "No one knows yer form yet. They gotta get a look at ya in the heats first."

"Is that right?"

"Fer Gawd's sake, Charlie, will ya stop worryin' about yer odds and start thinkin' about yer heat? Ya gotta be in the first three ta make the final, remember?"

"I remember, Mr. Redmond. First three."

After finding a spot away from the crowd, I began warming up with a few simple stretches. I hadn't run for a while, and my legs felt strong and fresh. As I sat on the grass, reaching for my toes, a pair of white running spikes walked by. It was the young man from the train.

"Rabbit Boy." He smirked. "I see you're in the first heat. Hope you've booked a seat on the early train home."

"Ignore 'im, Charlie," said Mr. Redmond, passing me a water bottle. "'Ere, 'ave a sip, then put yer spikes on."

I took up a spot near my bag and began untying the laces on my father's boots. For a moment I was back sitting on his bed again. I remembered his skeleton arms and how they'd struggled with the weight of the boots as he passed them to me. Maybe my father had known something way back then. Maybe he'd planned all along to be here with me—here when the stakes were high, when I needed him most.

I placed the boots into my bag and slipped my feet into the black spikes.

"Awright, Charlie." Mr. Redmond clapped me on the back. "Go fer a light trot and see 'ow they fit."

After the weight of my father's boots, I trotted off as if I was barefoot. Although my pace was easy, I could feel the metal spikes piercing the dirt and pushing me forward. I'd never felt so fast.

"They're beaut, Mr. Redmond," I breathed, having made my way back. "I'll be flyin' in 'em."

"Good lad."

If only he knew what I had planned.

Near the starting line, off to our left, a man in a white coat began ringing a bell.

"Runners fer heat one!" he called. "Runners fer heat one!"

Mr. Redmond moved close to me and put an arm around my shoulders. I was unable to meet his eyes, so I kept my head down and stared at the grass.

"Awright, Charlie, this is it. . . . Just remember, yer've done everythin' I asked of ya, and more. Yer ready fer this race, more than most of the runners 'ere. Now it's up ta you. Just remember what I told ya last night—if ya 'ave ta go wide, do it in the straight, but stay on the inside lane on the bends. Awright, give us ya coat, and I'll see ya back 'ere. Good luck, Charlie."

"Thanks, Mr. Redmond, I'll do me best."

"Good lad."

At the starting line I was the smallest of the runners by far. As the others limbered up, I sat on the oval beside the track and undid the laces on my spikes.

"Awright, fellas," called the official. "Let's make a start."

In what could have well proven to be the worst mistake of my life, I removed one shoe, then the other, and placed them on the grass. Barefoot, I joined the others on the diagonal starting line.

In the distance I could hear Mr. Redmond calling my name. "Charlie! What the flamin' 'eck are ya doin', lad? Put yer spikes on. Charlie!"

Without turning, I stood with the others on the line and shook my legs.

"Charlie!"

Beside the track, the official moved into place.

"I won't start yas till yer behind the line, lads."

Happy with the line, he raised a starter's gun high in the air.

"Awright . . . take yer marks . . . set . . ."

Bang!

We were off.

I jumped from the middle of the line and went toward the inside lane. Just as Mr. Redmond had predicted, the going was immediately rough. While the other runners used their bulk to find a position, I called on my speed and managed to settle midway in the pack, on the inside lane. We went like that for one lap, then two, at a surprisingly easy pace. Then, on the third lap, it happened—a bolter broke away in a desperate attempt to lead, but was soon reeled in by the main group. Three laps. At the start of the fourth, runners began to make their moves. As

we took the second to last bend, I held my spot inside and resisted the urge to go wide. Those who did paid the price and
soon began to struggle in the straight. One more bend. Again
they went wide. Still midfield, I felt comfortable, so I quickened my pace and moved forward into the final straight. As
soon as we hit it, I stepped wide and ran. Without my spikes, I
called on every bit of strength and somehow managed to make
up ground on the leaders. It was a dangerous game I was playing, but I started counting the runners in front. There were
four. One more spot and I was home. I didn't want to win. I
wanted to be third. Gaps began to open up between the four
runners, so I settled in behind the first two and crossed the line.

I was third, and through to the final.

Mr. Redmond, who was hovering at the finishing line, ran
toward me and threw his arms around me.

"Yer in, Charlie!" he screamed. "Ya made the final!"

As quick as he'd been to congratulate me, the celebration
stopped.

"Now would ya mind tellin' me what the flamin' 'eck ya
were doin' runnin' barefoot?"

Doubled over, I sucked in air, barely able to talk.

"I'm sorry ta go behind ya back like that, Mr. Redmond, but
would ya mind if I told ya later?"

The three of us, first, second, and third, were taken to the
bookies' tent, where our names were recorded on a board.
When I gave my own name, the gent writing the names looked
up and laughed.

"Charlie Feehan?" he chuckled. "Yer the lad what ran barefoot, aren't ya?"

"I am, sir."

"I seen a lot a things in me time, lad, but I never seen a runner run barefoot in a professional footrace. I 'ate ta spoil yer fun, Charlie Feehan, but ya ain't got a 'ope in 'ell."

As I turned my back on a chorus of laughter, I threw Mr. Redmond a wink, then steered him away from the crowd.

"What's goin' on, Charlie?" he asked.

"If there's one thing I learnt, Mr. Redmond, when I was workin' fer Squizzy Taylor, it's never ta show yer strength before a fight."

"Eh?"

"Did ya hear 'em laughin' back there?"

"I 'eard 'em awright."

"It's exactly what I was 'opin' fer."

"It was?"

"That's right. I don't know if yer gunna like what I'm up ta, Mr. Redmond, but I ran barefoot ta give me odds a boost."

"Ya what?"

Mr. Redmond looked at me, stunned. "And 'ow did ya know ya were gunna even make it through? Ya could a missed the final with a stunt like that."

"I'm sorry, Mr. Redmond. I know 'ow much yer've 'elped me, but this race, it's me chance fer somethin' better."

Sensing his confusion, I put my arm around his shoulders and steered him farther afield. After a cautious look left and then right, I pulled the envelope from my pocket and handed it to him.

"In that there envelope is twenty-three quid," I whispered. "As soon as the odds are posted after the final heat, I want ya ta put the lot on me nose."

"Twenty-three quid? 'Ave yer lost yer mind, lad?"

"Please, Mr. Redmond."

"Jaysus, lad, yer only sixteen. I won't do it. It's a mug's game, gamblin'. Twenty-three quid is more money than most people see in a lifetime. Yer mother'd 'ave a fit if she knew what ya were askin'. And yer father, what would he say, Charlie?"

Over and over I'd thought my plan through in my head, and every time I'd come to the same conclusion.

"Look, Mr. Redmond," I said, "I know well enough what gamblin' can do ta a family. I seen families ripped apart. Workin' fer Squizzy Taylor, I seen it all. I've seen the two-up schools, the sly groggers, the brothels, none of it pretty at all. And that money I just gave yer now, it's money earned from the likes a that. It's dirty money, Mr. Redmond. It's all me savin's runnin' fer Squizzy Taylor. I want ta use it fer somethin' good."

"Give it ta yer mother, then."

"No."

"Charlie, ya could blow the lot."

"Ya don't think I can win, is that it?"

"A course not, Charlie. D'ya think I'd be 'ere if I thought that?"

The two of us were now standing in the middle of the oval a few yards apart, oblivious to the second heat being run around us.

"Look, Mr. Redmond, I ain't proud a 'ow I earned the money. But I need ya ta do this fer me."

In front of me, Mr. Redmond shook his head and ran his fingers through his hair.

"Jaysus, lad, I 'ope ya know what yer doin'."

As he spoke the words, he took one last look into my eyes, then dropped the envelope into his pocket.

"C'mon, then," he said. "We got a race ta win."

Even though I'd made up my mind what to do with the money a few days before, I don't mind admitting that the very thought of losing it terrified me. It was a sum and a half, after all. But at the same time, knowing where it came from, I felt somewhat relieved to no longer have it with me. I have no doubt that if the money had been earned through honest means, I no sooner would have gambled it than taken to it with a match. Yes, the stakes were high, but money-wise, I had nothing to lose.

As soon as I began warming up for the final, I pushed the money from my mind. Even when Mr. Redmond returned from the bookies' tent with sweat on his brow, I continued on in silence. I was here to run.

After composing himself, Mr. Redmond took a sip of water, then offered me the bottle. "I take it yer've no more tricks up yer sleeve, Charlie?" he asked.

"No more, Mr. Redmond. I'm 'ere ta run."

"I'm glad ta 'ear it, lad. And ya'll be doin' the runnin' in spikes, I take it?"

"A course. It's the final, Mr. Redmond. I ain't that stupid."

"Very well. How are yer legs feelin'? Why don't ya lie down and I'll give 'em a rub."

I did as instructed, and soon Mr. Redmond was working his knuckles into my right calf. After my left, he moved on to my thighs until my legs were tingling all over.

"Awright, then, Charlie," he said. "Pull on yer spikes and we'll go fer a trot."

Still in my coat, I jogged across the oval nice and easy. Runners passed by me in flashy colors, among them the man from the train. His singlet was a shiny maroon color with a gold emblem blazoned across his chest. Me, I wore a white singlet and a pair of brown shorts that scratched at my inner thighs when I ran. When he saw me, he slowed to a jog.

"You made the final, I see, Rabbit Boy," he said. "Must've been an easy heat you were in. See you on the line."

Soon enough, the starter began ringing his bell.

"Runners fer the final!" he called. "Runners fer the Ballarat Mile!"

This time, Mr. Redmond walked me over to the starting line.

"Get yerselves ready, lads," called the starter. "We're gettin' close ta time."

A little way from the rest of the runners, Mr. Redmond once again put a hand on my shoulder and looked deep into my eyes.

"This is it, Charlie," he said. "The Ballarat Mile."

I gritted my teeth and returned his gaze.

"Don't be fooled by these bigger fellas 'ere," he continued. "It don't mean nothin' bein' big, ya saw that in the heat. Fink smart, Charlie, and run yer own race."

Slowly his hand moved from my shoulder to my face. With tears in his eyes, he drew me in and kissed my cheek.

"Good luck, Charlie," he sniffed. "Make me proud."

As I handed him my coat, an envelope dropped from a pocket onto the grass. With everything that had happened, I'd completely forgotten it was there. I picked it up and slid a single sheet of paper from it.

Dear Charlie,

Run like the wind.

Love, Alice

Now I was ready to run.

I handed Mr. Redmond the note, then joined the others at the start. Left foot forward, I stood on the line and drove the spikes of my shoes down into the dirt.

"Very well, lads," called the starter. "This is it—the final of the Ballarat Mile. I'm ready fer yis. Make a line, if ya will."

From the corner of my eye I saw him raise the gun in the air.

"Take yer marks . . . set . . ."

Bang!

I jumped from the line better than most and once again headed straight for the inside. Fourteen others had the same idea, and soon I was caught in a pack, bumping and jostling for position. At the first bend I was running three wide to avoid being knocked to the ground by the bigger runners, who'd by now settled inside. Try as I might, no one would let me in. Mr. Redmond must have been close by, for I could hear him shouting instructions.

"Get inside, Charlie! Fer Gawd's sake, get yerself inside!"

Down the back straight I tried again, but the runners were too tightly packed. Covering more ground than the inside runners, I began to fall back a few spots until I was midfield again. As a runner on my left swung wide in the straight, I finally slipped inside and found some rhythm. Once there, I was able to get a feel for the pace. It was quick, much quicker than the earlier heat, and after the first lap I began to wonder whether I'd be able to keep it up. For the time being, however, I was happy enough to stay put midfield and wait. Although there'd been little change in the order, after lap two the pace, thankfully, had slackened. Lap three, I decided, was the time to make my move. As we rounded the bend into the back straight, I moved out a lane and overtook two, maybe three runners, then slipped back to the inside lane. Up ahead I spotted a maroon singlet running second. One lap to go.

At the start of the final lap, I realized that the race would be decided in the final straight. Currently, however, I was in no position to threaten the leaders once we arrived. I needed to move, and I needed to do it now. On the third-to-last bend I stayed inside, then as soon as we hit the straight I bolted. Behind, I felt someone come with me, so I maintained my pace. At the next bend I was in lane two with a runner on my left and one on my right. A whole pack of them had moved with me down the straight, and suddenly there were half a dozen trying to run wide. Quickly the widest runners began to slow, until I found myself alongside the maroon singlet. Someone joined us on my right, making it four of us in a line. This was it. The winner of the Ballarat Mile was about to be decided.

After four grueling laps, the race had come down to a sprint. Into the straight, although my legs were burning, I called on them for more, and they responded. On my inside the maroon singlet came with me, until it was just the two of us heading for the line. Then suddenly, something strange happened. Lane two lit up in front of me, and as I looked to the line, for a moment I saw a group of people cheering me on—my father, my ma, Jack, Alice, and Nostrils. They were all there.

When I saw them, my legs seemed to find something more. With a heaving chest I ran toward them, a flash of maroon by my side, and lunged desperately across the line.

For a few seconds I was not sure who had won, but when I saw Mr. Redmond running toward me with his arms in the air, I knew it was me.

"Wahoooo!"

When he got to me, he lifted me up in his arms and spun me around so many times I thought I might be sick. Over and over he kept screaming the same thing. "Ya just won the Mile, Charlie! Ya just won the Mile!"

By the time he put me down, I was able to string a few words together. I put my arms around his neck and hugged him tight.

"*We* won the Mile, Mr. Redmond," I said. "*We* won the Mile. I couldn't a done it without ya."

After Mr. Redmond, the first to congratulate me was the official in the white coat.

"Well done, lad," he said with a smile, offering me his hand. "I think ya just wrote yerself inta the 'istory books. Ya'd 'ave ta be the youngest winner of the Mile, I reckon. Anyway, 'ow'd ya like ta walk a victory lap fer us?"

Grabbing hold of Mr. Redmond's arm, I forced him to walk a lap with me around the track. As we made our way around the outside lane, a string of people darted from the crowd to shake my hand and pat my back. I could hardly believe it.

"Fancy that, eh, Mr. Redmond?" I said. "I'm the youngest runner ta win the Mile."

"And that ain't all, I'll 'ave ya know. By my reckonin', Charlie, ya might just be the richest, too." His voice was quavering. "I put yer money on yer nose. Just like ya asked."

"And?"

"And I got ya at fifty ta one."

"'Struth!"

"'Struth is right. If me sums is right, with the prize money an' all, yer've a grand total in yer kitty of one thousand two hundred pound."

As I let out a scream, two men picked me up and put me on their shoulders. I was King Charlie and this was my moment.

In the crowd I spotted Mrs. Pickwick, who raised her hand to her mouth and blew a kiss from her palm. She'd been right after all—the black running spikes she'd seen in her dreams belonged to me.

After the victory lap, we headed toward the crowd gathered in front of the white marquees, where I was presented with a silver cup and the fifty-quid purse. The Ballarat Mile of 1919 had been run and won, and my name, Charlie Feehan, was written in the books as the youngest runner ever to win.

I continued shaking hands until Mr. Redmond appeared sometime later and put his hand on my shoulder. He smiled, then with his free hand patted the huge bulge of money in his coat pocket.

"Giddyup." He winked. "I don't want ta spoil yer fun, Charlie, but we got a train ta catch."

Although I was enjoying the attention, I shook a few more hands, then followed Mr. Redmond through a cheering crowd. I couldn't wait to get back home—back to Ma and Jack.

After we packed our things, Mrs. Pickwick met us at her front door with a bag of fresh veggies. She handed them to me and kissed my cheek.

"If ya ever enter the Mile again, Charlie, ya be sure ta come and stay. It was a pleasure 'avin' ya 'ere."

"Thanks, Mrs. Pickwick. I reckon that stew ya cooked last night might a got me over the line."

"No fear, Charlie. I've 'ad a few runners stay with me over the years, and I can tell ya, without a shadow of a doubt, ya won that race on yer own."

CHAPTER TWENTY-TWO

I was just as excited to be returning home as I had been on the train trip up. As I sat on a leather seat, gazing out the window, I heard a familiar voice behind me.

"Charlie Feehan?"

When I turned, the runner from the Melbourne Harriers, the young man I'd pipped on the line, stood before me with a bag slung over his shoulder.

He stepped forward and offered me his hand.

"You sure can run, Charlie Feehan."

"Thanks."

"You were right about the speed, too. . . . I've never heard of rabbiting as a training method, but if I'm ever down at Yarra Park, I'll keep my eyes out for you."

"No worries."

"And if you're ever thinking of training with a club, we'd love to have you at the Harriers."

"Thanks all the same, but I got a trainer right 'ere."

"Suit yourself. Anyway, good luck, and who knows— I might see you next year."

"Who knows—ya just might."

The two of us shook hands again, only this time, instead of taking the seat opposite, the young man slid into a seat a few rows up. Beside me, Mr. Redmond sat nervously, a hand guarding the wad of money in his coat pocket.

"So then, Charlie," he said quietly. "What are ya gunna do with it all?"

"I'm glad ya asked, Mr. Redmond. Funnily enough, it's somethin' that I'm gunna need yer help with."

During the trip home, I told Mr. Redmond all about my secret plans. The technicalities he'd look into, but as far as he could tell, the problems were bound to be few.

"As ya know yerself, Charlie," he said, "money talks like nothin' else."

"So ya'll organize it fer me, then?"

"A course I will. Why don't ya 'ave a snooze? Go on, ya bloody well earnt it, I reckon."

As we walked home from the station, my eyes gobbled up the city sights. All around me things were on the move. There were noises everywhere.

I turned to Mr. Redmond and smiled.

"Ain't it good ta be 'ome, Mr. Redmond?"

"That it is, Charlie," he replied. "That it is."

Finally the two of us turned into Cubitt Street and continued on until we reached my front gate. As we slowed to a halt, I pulled the silver cup from my bag and handed it to him.

"Here, Mr. Redmond. I want ya ta 'ave this."

"No, Charlie, I can't."

"I can show it ta me ma in the mornin', Mr. Redmond. I want ya ta 'ave it."

"Charlie . . ."

"It ain't just the runnin', Mr. Redmond. Ya done so much fer us, I don't know where we'd be without ya."

Even in the dark of night, the silver cup seemed to have a brilliant shine about it. Slowly, Mr. Redmond raised it as if he was a priest lifting a chalice at Sunday Mass.

"'First place,'" he read. "'The Ballarat Mile, 1919.' God bless yer, Charlie. If I die in me sleep tonight, then I'll die a 'appy man."

"Don't ya go dyin' on me just yet," I said. "There's somethin' else I want ya ta do first."

"There is?"

"Yeah. I want ya ta take whatever ya need from the winnin's and see about a new set a teeth fer Mrs. Redmond. Whatever it takes, Mr. Redmond. The cost don't worry me none."

"But, Charlie . . ."

For the first time in his life, Mr. Redmond was lost for words. I stepped forward and hugged him to me.

"Finkin' and footwork," I whispered in his ear. "Finkin' and footwork."

Inside, our house felt deliciously warm. Ma must have heard me at the door, for in seconds she was standing before me in the hall, silent, her eyes doing the asking instead of her mouth.

"I won it, Ma," I said.

Before she had time to move, I stepped forward and fell into her arms.

CHAPTER TWENTY-THREE

At eleven o'clock on Saturday, two weeks after the Balla-rat Mile, I met with my invited guests outside the gate of Porter's Wood Yard, in Church Street, Richmond. They were all there: Ma, Jack, the Redmonds, Alice and her father, Mr. and Mrs. Heath, and of course Nostrils. Besides Mr. Redmond and myself, no one had a clue why they were there.

At a few minutes past eleven, the time had finally come to put the bewildered guests out of their misery. Mr. Redmond and I positioned ourselves on either side of the newly erected sign that we'd earlier covered with a huge black sheet.

"C'mon, Charlie," he whispered. "Get a wriggle on, will ya? There's some nasty cumulus formin' over'ead."

"Awright, Mr. Redmond." I smiled. "Keep yer shirt on."

Clearing my throat, I turned and faced the small crowd.

"Awright, then," I announced. "I s'pose yer all wonderin' why I've invited yas all 'ere. Well, yer about ta find out. Nostrils, if ya can work them crutches 'oldin' ya up, I'd like ya ta come out 'ere and do the honors, if ya will."

Surprisingly, Nostrils managed to cover the few yards without too much fuss until he was standing beside me, a confused look on his face.

I handed him the drawstring connected to the sheet, then waved my arm to indicate the yard behind me.

"Ladies and gentlemen, I give you . . ."

Nostrils may have been an expert bell ringer, but he was nothing when it came to pulling a drawstring. Not wanting to cause a scene, I leaned sideways and whispered in his ear.

"Fer Gawd's sake, Nostrils, will ya give the bloody thing a tug?"

With his right hand, Nostrils yanked at the drawstring. As the black sheet fell from the sign, I turned once again to face my guests, then waved an arm behind me.

"Ladies and gentlemen, I give ya the Heath and Feehan Timber Company!"

From my coat pocket, I grabbed hold of a set of keys and tossed them to Nostrils.

"Seems only fair," I told him with a smile. "Seein' as yer've got top billin'."

Nostrils stood completely still, staring at the keys in his hand.

"Bloody 'ell, Charlie," he managed.

"Come on, Nostrils, will ya open the bloody gate? We got people 'ere wantin' a tour."

In the small but comfortable office, as Mr. Redmond began explaining the workings of the yard, someone's hand gripped my right shoulder. It was Mr. Heath.

"I've lost count a how many F's we're up ta, Charlie," he said, "but I never in me whole life seen a finer friend than yerself."

"I don't know about that, Mr. Heath," I replied. "I reckon I got a bit ta make up fer."

.   .   .

When Mr. Redmond was finished playing tour guide, Ma invited the guests back for refreshments at our house in Cubitt Street. When we arrived at the front gate, a familiar song was playing inside.

I'm forever blowing bubbles,
Pretty bubbles in the air. . . .

Mrs. Redmond, who'd been dispatched home early by her husband, had the place set for a party. There was beer and lemonade and, on a side table near the window, enough cakes and pastries to feed a footy team. In fact, had we been asked to take the field, I'm sure we would've had the numbers. Instead, the whole lot of us danced. We crammed into that tiny room like we used to when my father was alive. Song after song we swapped partners, until it came my turn to dance with Alice. At first the two of us stood at a polite distance, but soon enough she drew me in so close that our cheeks touched and her hair tickled my nose. At that moment, as I breathed her in, it was as if we were the only ones in the room.

Halfway through the song, a wetness on my cheek made me pull away. I looked at Alice and saw that she was crying.

"What's wrong, Alice?" I whispered. "Am I steppin' on yer toes?"

"No, Charlie," she sniffed. "I'm just lookin' at me dad. He's dancin', Charlie. . . . I can't believe me eyes. It's the first time I ever seen him dance."

As she wiped her eyes, I stepped back and took a quick look over my shoulder.

"Maybe ya should go and—"

Before I'd finished, I felt her hands pull me close again.

"Ah, no ya don't," she said. "I ain't givin' ya up just yet."

.　.　.

We danced and sang well into the night until the only guests left were Mr. and Mrs. Redmond.

As Mr. Redmond sat in the corner of the living room drinking beer from the Ballarat Cup, I ducked off into the hall and headed for the door.

As I turned the knob, Ma appeared behind me.

"Where are ya goin', Charlie?" she asked.

"I'm goin' runnin', Ma."

"Runnin'? Where to?"

I dropped my eyes to my father's boots, then looked up and smiled.

"Who knows, Ma. Who knows."

AUTHOR'S NOTE

While this is a work of fiction, some of the characters in this story are real—Squizzy Taylor, the notorious Richmond crime boss, and his lover, Dolly; Henry Stokes, the famous two-up king; and Snowy Cutmore, a Fitzroy criminal and the man who reportedly shot Squizzy dead. All of the other characters are fictitious.

In 1919, Richmond was also known as "Struggletown." For many families, surviving was a tricky business. They lived life day to day and hand to mouth, struggling to make the most of measly pickings. The Feehan family is typical of many that lived in the working-class slums of Richmond. So while aspects of this novel are both real and imagined, it must be said that, most importantly, this is Charlie Feehan's story. This is his struggle, and his struggle is real.

GLOSSARY

ARVO: Afternoon. (This word illustrates the Australian tendency to shorten even the most mundane words.)

BLOCKS: Refers to "starting blocks," the equipment athletes use to assist them at the start of a race.

BROLLY: An umbrella.

BUCKLEY'S: Means "no chance." Derived from William Buckley, a convict who settled in Australia. Buckley escaped into the bush near the seaside settlement of Sorrento. The bush was inhabited by the native aborigines, and Buckley, being a white man, had "no chance" of surviving. Surprisingly enough, the aborigines took him in, and he lived among them for a long time. Many years later, Buckley returned to the settlement and was employed as an interpreter, helping in the communication between the white settlers and the aborigines.

FAIR DINKUM: Honestly, seriously.

FOOTY: Footy is Australian Rules football, a fast-paced, physical game with eighteen players on each side. It is a free-flowing game, played on an oval-shaped grass field. The ball is also oval-shaped and is made from leather. The idea is to move the ball, by either kicking or hand-passing (punching the ball with a clenched fist), to teammates around the field with the objective of kicking it through the goals at either end. The goals consist of four posts—two larger posts in the center and two smaller ones on either side. Kicking the ball through the larger posts scores six points, and kicking it through the smaller ones scores one point. The game is broken down into four quarters, each quarter lasting around twenty minutes, not taking into account overtime. Players can run with the ball but must bounce it on the ground in front of them. A good footy team will have a combination of taller, medium, and smaller players, as there are different skills required to play the game.

GOING THE KNUCKLE: Punching someone, beating someone up, working someone over.

GO LIKE THE CLAPPERS: To run very fast, to move quickly. Derived from a clapper—the metal ball inside a bell that, when moved vigorously from side to side, makes contact with the outer shell of the bell to produce the ding.

HANDIES: Holding hands.

HIT IT CLEAR FOR SIX: A cricketing term, similar to a home run in baseball. When the ball is hit over the fence in cricket, the batter is awarded six points.

NO STRANGER TO THE CLARET: Describes a hard man, often a criminal type, or someone who is good with his fists and enjoys spilling blood, preferably not his own.

NUGGET: Shoe polish.

PUNTER: Someone who likes to gamble or bet.

PUSH: A gang.

RIDGY-DIDGE: Really, honestly, genuine.

ROVER: A smaller footy player whose job is to run the ball, or move it quickly forward by either kicking or hand-passing to a teammate.

RUCKMAN: The tallest player on the footy field. The game commences with an umpire bouncing the ball in the center of the oval. It is the ruckman's job to jump up and tap the ball to the smaller, running players (rovers). A feature of the game is the overhead marking, or catching the ball. The ruckman is particularly skilled at this, as he has the height to tower over his smaller opponents.

SHEILA: A girl or woman.

SLY GROGGER: Someone who supplies illegal liquor after hours. Liquor and beer could be legally bought before six o'clock. However, it was illegal to sell them after that time. Sly groggers supplied liquor and beer after hours for parties and for those that ran dry.

SP BOOKMAKER: An illegal, off-course bookmaker who takes bets. At the racetrack, a horse's odds often fluctuate prior to the race, so *SP* refers to *starting price*—the odds of a horse when it starts the race. The *starting price* is the dividend the punter is paid.

STOUSH: A fight.

TAKING THE MICKEY: Mocking.

TAKING THE PISS: Joking, kidding.

TICKETS ON YOURSELF: Fancying yourself, thinking you're special.

TWO-UP SCHOOL: An illegal form of gambling employing the two-up game, in which a "spinner" tosses two coins, with heads on one side and tails on the other, into the air. It is possible for the coins to fall in a number of combinations when they hit the ground (i.e., two heads, two tails, a head and a tail), and punters will lay bets accordingly. These games were often rowdy spectacles.

ABOUT THE AUTHOR

Robert Newton, the son of an army officer, spent his childhood moving to different postings around Australia. Six schools later, including a stint in Singapore, his family finally settled in Melbourne. After completing school, Robert spent the next few years studying at university, traveling, and trying his hand at various jobs. He decided to become a full-time firefighter, and has been in the Metropolitan Fire Brigade for sixteen years.

When he's not putting out fires, Rob likes to surf and write, and he has a black belt in karate. He is the author of several young adult novels, and this is his first to be published in the United States. He lives in Melbourne with his wife and three daughters.

COCHRAN PUBLIC LIBRARY
174 BURKE STREET
STOCKBRIDGE, GA 30281